mary-kateandashley

Sweet 16

Danielle F

4/5

mary-kateandashley

Sweet 16
THE PERFECT SUMMER

Kieran Scott

📕 HarperCollins*Entertainment*
An Imprint of HarperCollins*Publishers*

A PARACHUTE PRESS BOOK

A PARACHUTE PRESS BOOK
Parachute Publishing, LLC
156 Fifth Avenue
Suite 325
NEW YORK
NY 10010

First published in the USA by HarperEntertainment 2002
First published in Great Britain by HarperCollins*Entertainment* 2002
HarperCollins*Entertainment* is an imprint of HarperCollins*Publishers* Ltd,
77-85 Fulham Palace Road, Hammersmith, London W6 8JB

SWEET 16 books are created and produced by Parachute Press, LLC, in
cooperation with Dualstar Publications, a division of Dualstar Entertainment Group,
LLC, published by HarperEntertainment, an imprint of HarperCollins Publishers.

The HarperCollins website address is
www.**fire**and**water**.com

1 3 5 7 9 8 6 4 2

The author asserts the moral right to be
identified as the author of the work.

ISBN 0 00 714881 X

Printed and bound in Great Britain by Clays Ltd, St Ives plc

chapter one

"Ashley! Have you seen my purple tank top?" I shouted. I yanked open my bottom dresser drawer and emptied the entire contents onto the floor.

"No! Sorry!" Ashley shouted back, her voice muffled. She was obviously in the back of her closet, doing the same thing I was – last-minute emergency packing for our summer away.

I sifted through the tangle of clothes, then looked around my room and sighed. The place was always a wreck, but today it was ten times messier than usual. My suitcase sat open in the middle of my bed with clothes spewing out of it. All the rejected items were strewn on the floor. My make-up case was packed to the brim and my backpack overflowed with magazines, hair products and pictures of my friends.

The tank top, of course, was nowhere in sight.

"I can't believe we're leaving today!" Ashley gasped. She ran into my room, her big blue eyes sparkling.

"I know!" I said. "This time tomorrow, we are going to be chillin' with rock stars."

"Living on our own!" Ashley added.

"Living on our own surrounded by *rock stars,*" I added.

Ashley perched on the edge of my bed. "I still can't believe Dad is letting us work at MusicFest."

"Yeah, tell me about it." I frowned with mock concern. "Do you think he's going senile?"

"Mary-Kate!" Ashley rolled her eyes. She picked up a piece of clothing from the floor and tossed it at me. It landed on my head, covering my face. I peeled it away. Oh, wow! My purple tank top.

"You found it!" I cheered, shoving it into my bag. "Now I'm almost ready."

"Good. I'm going to go put my stuff in the car. I'll meet you downstairs!" Ashley nearly skipped out of the room.

I went back to packing. I was totally kidding about that senile comment – but it really *had* come as a shock when Dad announced that he'd found summer jobs for Ashley and me at a huge music festival.

Dad works for a record company and constantly

hangs with all these way cool people, but he's never let Ashley and me within three miles of anyone famous. He makes a point of keeping his family separate from his job.

But I guess when he heard about this MusicFest opportunity, he realised it was too good to pass up. Ashley and I would be spending a month living in the dorms at Trager University, going to free concerts, meeting new people . . . and, oh, yeah, working a little.

Satisfied that I finally had everything, I zipped my suitcase shut, grabbed all my bags and lugged them downstairs.

My parents were outside, leaning on the Mustang convertible they had given Ashley and me as a sweet sixteen gift. Looking at the shiny pink car still gave me goose bumps. I couldn't believe it was ours!

"Have I mentioned recently that you guys are the coolest parents ever?" I said. I struggled to lift my bags into the backseat next to Ashley's.

"No, not recently," Dad joked. He gave Mom's shoulder a little squeeze.

"I mean, first you let us throw the biggest, most amazing sweet sixteen party ever, then you get us a car, and now you're letting us go away for an entire month." I put my hands on my hips. "I really think there should be an award for this kind of behaviour."

"Well, you're about to think we're even cooler," Dad said. He reached into the passenger seat of our car and pulled out two brand-new mobile phones – one was shiny silver. The other one was metallic purple.

"Are you kidding me?" I exclaimed. I grabbed the silver one. I knew Ashley would totally love the purple.

"We weren't going to let you leave without a way of contacting us in an emergency," Mom said.

"Thank you, guys, *so* much!" I cried. "Now I can call Jake and Brittany and Lauren—"

"I said emergencies," Mom corrected me. She gave me a big bear hug. "I'm going to miss you!"

"I'm going to miss you, too!" I answered.

"Mary-Kate!" Ashley called from the house. "Telephone! It's Jake!"

My heart gave a little flop. I ran back to the house, slipping my new mobile in my pocket.

Jake Impenna was this amazing, gorgeous, sensitive, athletic, soon-to-be-senior whom I started dating last spring after a ton of misunderstandings. First I invited him to our sweet sixteen party. Then I uninvited him and he thought I didn't like him. Then I invited him again... It was a huge mess! But it ended with Jake and me totally happy together.

"Wait till you see what Mom and Dad got us!" I whispered to Ashley as I took the phone from her. She grinned and jogged outside.

"Hey," I said to Jake. I tucked my long blonde hair behind my ear as I walked into the living room.

"Hey," he said quietly. The sound of his voice made my skin tingle. I could tell he was already missing me. I had to admit I was missing him, too. "I just wanted to call to say good-bye again and . . . you know . . . wish you luck."

"Thanks." I walked slowly around the couch. "I'll call you as soon as I get there."

"Cool," Jake said. "So listen, don't fall in love with any rock stars while you're there, okay?"

"I promise I won't," I answered. "Unless, of course, I meet Gavin Michaels. Then I can't be responsible for my actions."

Gavin was the eighteen-year-old lead singer of my favourite band, Glowstick, and everyone knew I had a massive crush on him.

"Ha ha," Jake said dryly. "Well, I'll miss you, Mary-Kate."

"I'll miss you, too, Jake." I squeezed my eyes shut, hard, to keep the tears back. "Bye."

"Bye," he whispered.

I hung up and just stood still for a second, feeling sorry for myself. Jake and I were so happy. It would have been great to spend the whole summer with him, going to the movies, hitting the beach, having picnics...

"Mary-Kate!" Ashley called from the front door. "Let's go! The rock stars are waiting for us!"

I laughed and snapped out of my funk. It wasn't like I was going to Alaska. I could talk to Jake as much as I wanted. And in the meantime Ashley and I would be living on our own, meeting fabulous people, and having the time of our lives.

I put the phone back in the kitchen and rushed outside to the car.

Let the fun begin!

"Oooh! We are so going to be late!" I glanced away from the road to check my watch.

"Ashley, can you please stop being Miss Responsible for one second and appreciate the tremendousness of this moment?" Mary-Kate said, tipping her head back to look up at the clear blue sky. "We're in our own car, cruising up the coast, heading for the coolest summer ever!"

"I know! I know." I gave myself a moment to savour the feel of my hair whipping around in the wind and the sun on my face. But it didn't last long. "Still, a lot of people have already been there for a week. This is the last day to check in, and if we're late—"

"We're not going to be late," Mary-Kate said, cutting me off. She pushed her purple-tinted sunglasses up on her head and grinned at me. "Come on, let's talk about something else. What do you think our jobs are going to be?"

"Maybe we'll get to be personal assistants to the stars," I said dreamily.

"Or maybe we'll both get to work in wardrobe, picking out costumes for all the acts," Mary-Kate suggested. "Whatever we do, I'm sure we're going to get to hang out with famous people."

"I know! And they're going to pay us to do it!" I added.

"What are you going to do with all the cash we're making this summer?" Mary-Kate asked.

"I am going to buy the Kentmore 2000 surround-sound stereo with ten-disc changer, dual-cassette deck and four remote speakers," I told her.

Mary-Kate stared at me as though I had just announced that I was going to buy myself a mail-order boyfriend.

"What?" I asked. "You can programme it to play forty hours of continuous music. I have the ad." I pointed at my crocheted bag, which sat at her feet.

Mary-Kate laughed as she leaned forward and pulled out the folded-up clipping. "Wow. You've put a lot of thought into this, haven't you?"

"I guess," I answered with a shrug. "I mean, I have wanted a stereo upgrade *forever*. So I'm going to sock away as much money as I possibly can this summer."

"Excellent," Mary-Kate said. "It's good to have a plan."

I cast her a sly look out of the corner of my eye. "You have no idea what you're going to buy, do you?"

My sister's attention span is a bit on the short side. Like last summer, one second she wanted to learn to surf and the next second she was all about scuba lessons, and the next second she moved on to horseback riding.

"I have some ideas." Mary-Kate adjusted her sunglasses. "I'm thinking of a new wardrobe, or maybe a DVD player for my room, or one of those new portable music players ... or maybe I'll get something for Jake..."

She trailed off with a little sigh. I could tell she missed her boyfriend already. What was it like? I wondered. What was it like to miss someone so much you could hardly bear to go away? Aside from my parents and my friends, I didn't have anyone special to miss this summer.

"Oh, no! Ashley!" Mary-Kate suddenly yelped.

"What?" I asked. I glanced in all of my mirrors. Was there a tractor-trailer bearing down on us?

"I think you just missed the turn-off!" Mary-Kate said. She grabbed the map and the directions from her lap and studied them.

"Oh, no." I gripped the steering wheel harder. "What do I do, Mary-Kate? What do I do?"

"Hold on... hold on..." She slapped the map with the back of her hand and moaned. "Yeah. We were supposed to take exit eighteen. We just passed exit twenty."

I tried not to panic. "I don't believe this. Our first big road trip and we're lost!" I thought of the new mobile phone nestled inside my bag. "Maybe we should call Mom and Dad."

"No way. This whole summer is supposed to be about us being independent!" Mary-Kate objected. "We can't call them for help when we've been away from home for only one hour!"

"Well?" I asked. "What do you suggest we do?"

"Stay calm," Mary-Kate said, looking over her shoulder. "We just have to turn around. Here! Take this exit! Maybe we can get back on the highway going in the other direction!"

"Okay . . . okay," I said shakily. I changed lanes. A car horn blared at us. I glanced in the rearview mirror.

"Sorry!" I called out. I had accidentally cut up an SUV behind me! A huge knot formed in my throat, but I managed to get on the exit ramp. At the top of the exit, all the signs were for unfamiliar towns.

"Now what?" I said. Cars were lining up behind us. One of them honked again and I yelped in surprise. "This isn't happening," I said, my palms starting to sweat.

"Okay, make a left," Mary-Kate said. "We have to get back on the highway. Maybe the entrance is over there."

I hit my blinker and made the left, but again, there were no signs for the highway. We were on a two-lane road, driving farther away from the road we wanted to be on.

"How far am I supposed to go?" I asked, glancing at Mary-Kate. She was starting to look a bit pale herself.

"There has to be a gas station somewhere." I could tell she was trying to sound calm. "We'll just stop and get directions."

"Okay." I forced myself to breathe evenly, but the road was lined with nothing but weeds and rocks as far as I could see. There were no signs of life anywhere!

"Oh! Stop there!" Mary-Kate cried out. She pointed at a little run-down building up ahead on the right.

I slowed down to check the place out. "You have to be kidding," I said. One of the windows was broken, the wooden door was all rotted, and it was marked by a hand-painted sign that simply said BAIT.

"That place has 'danger' written all over it," I insisted.

"Ashley, come on! We have to stop somewhere!" Mary-Kate argued.

"Not there," I said, hitting the gas.

"What are you doing?" Mary-Kate shouted as we sped by.

"There has to be another place," I replied.

Of course I was wrong. Fifteen minutes later the road we were on grew rocky, then it turned to dirt. Finally we saw a worn-down sign for a state park.

"Well . . . there you go." I smiled weakly. "People have to be in the park, right?"

The road opened up in front of us into a small parking lot. Along the far side was a rickety wooden fence, and on the other side of the fence was a sharp drop. I had driven us right to the edge of a cliff.

"Uh... nice view," I said, putting the car in park.

"This is a state park?" Mary-Kate asked, looking around at the deserted area. "I think Mom and Dad should check on where their tax dollars are going."

I groaned and buried my face in my hands. I couldn't believe this was happening. We were lost, we were late, and we had no idea how to get back on the main highway.

The best summer of our lives was definitely off to a not-so-promising start.

chapter two

"Look, Mary-Kate!" I cried. "We're saved!" As we drove away from the park, I spotted a little old man walking along the side of the road. He carried a tackle box and a couple of fishing rods. "Let's ask him how to get back to the main highway."

I pulled over near the old man. "Excuse me," Mary-Kate began. "Can you tell us how to get on" – she picked up the directions and looked them over – "Route 57 north?"

The man stared blankly at us for a moment. A *long* moment.

"Uh... sir?" I said.

"Well... sure, I can tell you that," the man said slowly. He pointed down the road. "Now... you want to go down here... and you'll see a left-hand turn just after a big rusted-out barrel—"

"Left-hand turn after a barrel," Mary-Kate said.

"Now... you don't want to take *that* turn—"

Mary-Kate looked at me. I shot her a glance that said *be patient*.

"And you don't want to take the *next* turn... but when you come to a fork in the road, you'll want to turn... *left*. Yes, left."

"Okay... " Mary-Kate said.

"Now, once you make that left, you're going to go about two... no... five... no... make that six or so miles and . . ."

I checked my watch. This could take all day. We were never going to get to MusicFest.

Ten minutes – ten *excruciating* minutes – later Mary-Kate had clear directions from the fisherman. We found our way back to the highway and I carefully merged into traffic.

"Okay, everything's going to be fine now," Mary-Kate said.

"Right," I answered. "How much longer until we get there?"

Mary-Kate looked down at the directions and then glanced at the clock.

"Another hour." She bit her bottom lip.

"And we're already an hour late," I said, shaking my head. "Let's just hope they don't fire us on sight."

"There it is!" An hour later, Mary-Kate pointed out the entrance to the Trager University campus. I was in a seriously bad mood. I was tired, I was hungry, and I was still upset over getting lost. I took a look around the campus. "Hey... this place is—"

"Totally cool?" Mary-Kate finished.

"Exactly." I grinned. Mary-Kate twisted around in her seat, taking in the huge stucco buildings, the winding paths and the beautiful flowers. Kids our age were everywhere, walking and talking, stringing up banners, and hauling instruments and amplifiers. The air buzzed with excitement.

"Whoa, Ashley, look at those guys!" Mary-Kate said under her breath. She grinned past me at a couple of cute older guys playing their guitars on a sprawling lawn.

"Hello? Have you already forgotten about Jake?" I joked.

"I meant for *you*!" Mary-Kate said quickly. "Look at those guys for *you*!"

I pulled the car into a parking space. Mary-Kate and I quickly unloaded our bags.

We hurried up a little hill, following the handwritten signs that read "MusicFest staff! Check in here!" I couldn't wait to find out where we were going to be living, not to mention what our jobs were.

The check-in table was set up in the middle of a huge lawn. But a bunch of workers were already packing it up. Oh, no! What if we were really in trouble? What if they gave away our jobs – or fired us or something? Mary-Kate marched right up to one of the girls and introduced herself.

"Hi! I'm Mary-Kate and this is Ashley." She put her bag down at her feet and lifted her hand in greeting. "Sorry we're late. We got a little lost."

The girl, who was Asian and really pretty, looked us over and smiled.

"Don't worry about it." She pushed her extremely long braid over her shoulder. "I'm always late for everything."

I sighed, relieved. We still had our jobs!

"I'm Akiko," she said, reaching out to shake hands with us. "Welcome to MusicFest. It's insane here. You're going to love it."

Mary-Kate and I laughed as Akiko looked up our names and housing assignments. An electric guitar blared out of an open window somewhere nearby. A few kids gathered in a circle on the grass, singing and dancing as a guy beat on a set of bongos. This place was definitely charged with musical energy!

"Okay, you guys are in Murray Hall," Akiko finally told us. She handed us a couple of keys and entry cards. She pointed over her shoulder. "Just follow that path up the hill halfway and you'll see it on your right. When you get there, find your dorm monitor, Mary-Beth. She's in room 105 and she'll give you your work assignments and all the other info."

"Thanks, Akiko," I said. I took the key with a smile, and Mary-Kate and I started up the path.

"Have fun!" Akiko called after us.

Don't worry – we plan to! I thought.

"Look at this place!" Ashley exclaimed as we walked into the lobby of our dorm.

There was a huge bulletin board across from the entrance with colourful lettering that read "Welcome All!" Beneath the letters were dozens of pictures of concerts and parties from last year's MusicFest. My jaw dropped when I saw all the cool people who had attended.

"Isn't that Spike from Jupiter Jones?" Ashley gasped, stabbing a finger at one of the photos. It showed a punked-out guy with a blue mohawk.

"It is," I confirmed, staring at the pictures. "And that's Melissa Ryan!" She was one of my favourite singers. "I've died and gone to heaven!"

"Come on," Ashley laughed. She headed for the door that led to the rooms. "We have to check in with Mary-Beth. I hope she's as nice as Akiko was."

The hallway was carpeted with newish blue rugs and the whole place smelled like fresh paint. I looked down at my key.

"We're in 122," I said.

"It should be right around this corner," Ashley

answered. "Yikes!" She stopped dead in her tracks – so quickly that I almost smacked right into her.

"Oh, hi," Ashley said tentatively.

An older girl with straight red hair and a serious scowl on her face stood in front of our room.

"*Finally,*" she huffed.

I shot a wary glance at Ashley.

"I'm guessing you're Ashley and Mary-Kate," she snapped.

"And you must be Mary-Beth." I flashed her my sweetest smile. "Is that our room?" I asked, moving to get around her. I was dying to put my stuff down.

"Yes." She glared at me as she blocked my way. "Aren't you a little late?"

Ashley began to apologise. "Yeah, sorry about that. We got lost and we—"

"Whatever," Mary-Beth interrupted. She shoved a stack of papers at each of us. "Here are your assignments, info on the cafeteria, the schedule, and everything else you'll need."

I dropped my bags and grabbed the papers excitedly. Mary-Beth can be as rude as she wants, I thought, scanning the papers. Just tell me what my work assignment is! Maybe I'll be a backstage make-up artist or coordinating costumes or—

"Food service?" Ashley asked.

I blinked down at my own assignment. "Stagehand? What does that mean?"

Mary-Beth smirked. "Basically it means you'll be lugging equipment around," she said. "And *you* will be working at the pizza stand," she told Ashley.

Ashley and I looked at each other, dumbfounded. So much for our glamorous summer jobs.

"Well, you better report to your assignments right away," Mary-Beth said, squeezing between us and starting off down the hall. "They were only expecting you two *hours* ago."

Ashley shot me a desperate pleading look. I knew we had to speak up about this now.

"Uh, Mary-Beth?" I said. She stopped and turned slowly to face us. "About these assignments, is there any way we can switch with someone else? We just thought—"

Mary-Beth laughed. "Maybe if you'd arrived here last week like the rest of us did… or if you'd even arrived on time *today*, you would have had some say in your assignments," she said. "But you didn't. So sorry but you're stuck."

With that, she walked around the corner. A couple of seconds later we heard a door slam.

"Yuck. Stuck with the Wicked Witch of the West as our dorm monitor," I said flatly.

Ashley sighed. I suddenly felt exhausted and disappointed. These jobs… and Mary-Beth… weren't exactly what we expected.

"Oh, well," Ashley said, trying to cheer us both up. "It can only get better from here – right?"

chapter three

"That girl is a serious downer," Mary-Kate said as I unlocked the door to our room.

"Well... maybe she's just having a bad day," I reasoned. I tried hard to stay optimistic, even though I was going to be selling pizza all summer.

I swung the door open and Mary-Kate's eyes immediately brightened.

"Check it out!" she cried, running past me into our room.

The room was spacious with two big closets and even bigger windows. The place was absolutely gleaming with sunlight. There were two beds, two large dressers, and a couple of desks with built-in bulletin boards.

"Hey! We have our own kitchen!" Mary-Kate said.

Along the back wall were a couple of cabinets, a tiny stove and a small fridge. She opened one of the cabinets and found a few plates, pots, pans and other random cooking equipment.

"This is so great!" I dropped my stuff in front of one of the closets and checked out the fridge. "We can keep water and juice and stuff—"

"And we can make our own meals!" Mary-Kate said, holding up one of the pots.

"We're going to have to hit the grocery store ASAP!" I added.

"Definitely," Mary-Kate said. She flung herself on to one of the beds and crossed her legs, looking up at the ceiling. "Home sweet home."

"I guess we should get ready for work." I opened one of my suitcases.

"Ugh!" Mary-Kate propped herself up on her elbows. "Hauling equipment around all summer? Well... maybe I can develop some muscle tone."

"There you go!" I said as I unfolded a T-shirt and started to change. "Try to look at the positive side. Our room is great and we are going to get to see all those performances for free."

"Exactly." Mary-Kate rummaged through one of her smaller bags. "We are the bright-side girls."

She pulled out her phone and sat down again, clicking it on.

"Ummm... bright-side girl?" I pulled the T-shirt over my head and lifted my hair out. "What are you doing?"

"I'm calling Mom and Dad to tell them we got

here okay," Mary-Kate said innocently. "And... *maybe* I was thinking about calling Jake."

I laughed as I grabbed my crocheted bag and my work assignment. "Just make it quick," I told her. "You don't want to be late on your first day... again!" I headed out of the door.

As I made my way across campus to the pizza stand, I couldn't believe what was going on around me. There was a whole shopping area with little vendors set up in canvas tents. They sold everything from concert T-shirts to beaded jewellery to pottery and bumper stickers. Out on the main lawn, little groups of people sat around, playing guitars and singing.

Everyone seemed so sophisticated. *And here I am,* I thought. *I'm one of them! All of these people are staff here, just like me. So that means I must be just like them – free to do what I want, cool, and...* mature! *Who cares about the pizza stand and the crazy drive and our even crazier dorm monitor. I'm here to have fun, and no matter what, I'm going to have it!*

I slowed my steps as I walked between the rows of food vendors, looking for the pizza stand. There was a kiosk selling hot dogs, another called "The Veggie Spot" with all-vegetarian meals, and a bunch of other places selling ice cream, lemonade, burgers – you name it!

21

By the time I found the pizza stand, I was sweating. It was really, really hot out. I reached up to push my hair away from my face and found my forehead dotted with sweat. Ugh! Just the way I wanted to look when I met my boss and co-workers!

Still, there wasn't much I could do. Two people were working the counter – a tall guy with jet-black hair and a pretty, petite, brunette girl who was helping a customer. I walked up and the guy greeted me with a bright smile.

"Can I help you?" he asked.

"Actually, I'm supposed to be working here," I said. "I'm Ashley."

"Oh! Nice to meet you! I'm Dennis," he said. "Come on in."

I walked around the counter and he opened a little half-door to let me in. The moment I stepped behind the counter, the already soaring temperature sky-rocketed. The heat coming off the pizza ovens was enough to make my hair frizz. I pulled the front of my shirt away from my stomach, hoping to cool off a little.

"It's not that bad. You'll get used to it after an hour or two," Dennis said kindly. "Listen, since it's your first day, you can just hand out the slices and sodas. I have to head out to a managers' meeting, so I'll teach you the register on your next shift. Okay?"

"Sounds good," I said.

"Penny!" Dennis called to the other worker. "This is Ashley. She's going to fill orders, so you ring while I'm gone."

"Sure," Penny said quietly. I smiled at her, but she quickly turned her attention to wiping down the counter.

"Good luck, Ashley," Dennis said. He walked off and disappeared into the crowd.

I looked around uncertainly, not sure where to stand or what to do.

"Wow. This place is like a sauna, huh?" I grinned at Penny, trying to break the ice.

She looked me over and didn't crack a smile. My grin faded. This girl wasn't giving me much to work with.

"So... where are you from?" I asked.

"I'm sure you've never heard of it," she said. Her tone told me she wasn't going to volunteer anything else.

Stung, I turned away. Penny was obviously not the Miss Congeniality of MusicFest. I looked down at my watch and sighed. Only three hours and fifty-six minutes left in my shift.

After I talked to Jake and changed my clothes, I jogged toward stage B.

"Hey! Do you know who's in charge around here?" I asked a short guy with dreadlocks.

"You found him!" he said, holding out his

hand to me. "I'm Theo, supervisor of this fine stage area. And you are... ?"

"So sorry I'm late," I answered, shaking his hand. "I'm Mary-Kate Olsen."

"It's a great pleasure to meet you, Mary-Kate." Theo smiled at me. "Olsen? That name sounds familiar. I know!" Theo snapped his fingers. "Are you related to the Olsen at Zone Records?"

"Yes, that's my dad," I explained. "He arranged for me and my sister to work here."

"Excellent." Theo nodded. "I've heard of your dad – the musicians like working with him. Anyway, I'm glad you're here, and don't worry about being late. Chris and Melinda over there will tell you what to do." He pointed at a truck next to the stage, where a guy and a girl were manoeuvring a large amp down to the ground.

"Thanks, Theo!" I said. I jogged over to the truck, glad that my boss was so nice.

"Hey! I'm Mary-Kate," I said. "You guys need help?"

"Yeah, actually," the girl answered. She had curly blonde hair that was pushed back from her face with a colourful scarf. She wore a pink tank top and denim shorts. "I'm Melinda," she said. "And this is my brother Chris."

"Hi there!" Chris said. "I would shake your hand, but I'm pretty grungy." He held up a sweaty palm and laughed.

"That's okay," I said. "So, what should I do?"

We spent the next half hour or so unloading equipment for a heavy metal band called Killer Turtles. I had never heard their music or even seen pictures of them. Heavy metal isn't my thing.

There were tons of people walking around the stage area. "So... which of these people are in the group?" I whispered to Chris and Melinda as we made our way from the stage back to the truck on one of our runs.

They laughed. "It's hard to tell," Chris said, running a hand over his shaggy blond hair. "Killer Turtles fans all dress just like the band!"

After about an hour of unloading, Theo walked by and told us we could take a break. There was a refreshment table set up behind the stage, and we attacked it. I was totally thirsty from all that hard work!

Chris, Melinda and I kicked back under a tree with some sodas and snacks. "So, Mary-Kate," Chris said. "How did you end up at MusicFest?"

"My dad," I replied, taking a sip of my soda. "He works for a record company, and when he heard they were looking for workers up here, he filled out applications for me and my sister as a surprise."

"Wow! That was so cool of him!" Melinda said. "My parents actually laughed when I showed them the application I got off the Internet."

"So how did you get them to let you come here?" I asked.

"We convinced them that a summer working away from home would look good on our college applications," Melinda said.

"It was definitely one of my better moments," Chris put in, leaning back on his elbows. "I knew that debate club practice would come in handy one day. But we're huge music fans, and we weren't going to miss seeing all these bands play. This is like, history in the making."

"Cool," I nodded. "What are your favourite bands?"

"Well, my sister is obsessed with a new pop band every week." Chris rolled his eyes at her. "Right now it's Glowstick, right? Or was that yesterday's pick?"

"I'm not *that* bad." Melinda whacked his arm. "At least I'm not a heavy metal fiend."

Chris hooked his arm around Melinda's neck and gave her a serious noogie as they both laughed. "Let's just say we have different tastes."

"Well, I'm going to have to side with Melinda and Glowstick," I told Chris. "I hope we can still be friends," I joked.

"Oh... I guess so," Chris replied. He held his hand up to shield the sun from his eyes as he looked at me. "So, are you going to come by the beach house tonight?"

"The beach house?" I asked, raising my eyebrows. "What's that?"

"It's so totally cool," Melinda gushed. "There's this old abandoned house on the shore, and the staff goes there every night to hang out."

"Yeah, there's usually a bonfire and music and dancing . . ." Chris added. "Plus tons of food."

"Sounds amazing!" I said with a grin. "My sister, Ashley, and I will definitely be there."

"Excellent!" Melinda said. "You'll love it!"

I sighed happily as I lay back in the grass. This beach-house thing sounded perfect. I couldn't wait to tell Ashley about it.

I hope the people Ashley's working with are as nice as Chris and Melinda, I thought. *I'm sure they must be. . . .*

"Here's your cola and here's your slice," I said, smiling. My brain had become kind of foggy in all the heat from the pizza stand.

"Thanks," my customer said before walking off.

I pushed a few wisps of hair away from my face and took a deep breath. In another half an hour I was out of here. I could not wait to take a shower and call it a night. It was hard staying energetic and customer-friendly when I was rapidly wilting. Not to mention that the person I was working with hadn't said a word to me in the last three hours.

"Hey, Penny!" someone called from behind me. "Plate delivery!"

Startled, I turned around to find a guy – an incredibly *cute* guy – coming in through the back of the stand with a few bags of paper plates and cups. He opened one of the cabinets and started putting stuff away. I couldn't help noticing his perfect tanned arms and sun-lightened brown hair.

When he stood up, he wiped his hands on the back of his jeans and smiled politely.

"Hi, I'm Ashley," I said.

"Hi," he said a bit timidly. "Brian."

He returned to organising the cabinets. I turned back to the counter with a huge grin plastered to my face. Apparently Brian was the strong, silent type!

"So, Penny," I said, suddenly feeling a bit more upbeat. "I never asked you... how did you end up working here?"

"I needed a job, so here I am," she said flatly.

I felt my face flush. Why didn't she want to talk to me?

It didn't matter. I wasn't ready to give up yet. "Are you... into music?"

"I have to refill the ice," Penny told me. She disappeared behind the ovens to raid the cooler.

For the first time in my life I wanted to yell at someone I didn't know. What was wrong with her? Couldn't she be just a little nice?

I glanced at Brian to see if he noticed our exchange. He shot me a sympathetic look. Still, I had to get out of there. I walked out of the back, behind the stand.

Whew! The air outside was about ten degrees cooler. A breeze hit my face and I began to feel better. Brian came out and stood beside me.

"Hey," he said. "Just hang in there. Penny will come around. It's your first day at a new job. It's supposed to stink."

He cracked a smile that I felt all the way down to my toes.

"Thanks," I said.

"It'll get better," he told me.

I smiled. He sounded so sure of himself that I believed him on the spot.

"See you around," Brian said as he headed off.

"Bye," I called after him.

As he walked away, I noticed that I was grinning – majorly grinning. Brian definitely had an effect on me.

Maybe there *would* be some upsides to this job!

chapter four

"I'm starving. I can't wait for dinner!" I said. Ashley and I walked into the dining hall. "Wow, it's practially empty in here," I noted.

There were a few people scattered at tables around the room. Otherwise, the place was dead.

Where was everybody? I wondered.

"So, meet any rock stars yet?" Ashley asked me as we grabbed a couple of trays.

I peered at the menu, checking out my choices. Shepherd's pie – no. Fried fish – double no. Meat loaf – yuck. "I met the Killer Turtles," I told her, taking a plate of pasta with tomato sauce.

"Who?" Ashley asked.

"Exactly," I replied.

Ashley laughed. "Well, I'm never going to meet anyone famous selling pizza all summer."

"Sure you will!" I told her. "We're the bright-side girls, remember? Besides, all those superstars eat nothing *but* pizza. Really. And you're going to be their supplier."

"Maybe," Ashley said.

Her shoulders were slumped and she was definitely dragging as we made our way across the dining hall to a table. She obviously hadn't had the best day. I felt bad for her, but at least I had some news that would cheer her up.

"So, guess what?" I said as we sat down at an empty table. "I met these really cool people, Melinda and Chris. They're brother and sister. They told me about this old beach house that the staff hangs out at every night. We *have* to go."

"Really?" Ashley's face brightened a bit. "What's it like?"

I twirled my fork into my pasta. "They said there's music and dancing and food and drinks. You know, standard party central."

"Sounds exactly like what I need," Ashley said.

"Didn't you meet anyone you liked today?" I asked.

"Well, there was this one guy, Brian." Ashley smiled slightly. "He seemed nice, but we barely got to talk."

"Cute?" I asked.

"Definitely," she said.

"So why so mopey?" I asked.

"The girl I work with, Penny, completely blew me off," Ashley explained, resting her cheek on her hand. "I don't think she likes me at all."

"Not possible," I said, taking a bite of my spaghetti.

The moment I tasted it, I frowned and grabbed my water. The pasta was cold and the sauce was terrible.

"What's wrong?" Ashley asked, scrunching her face up as she watched me try to swallow.

"No wonder there's no one here," I said. "It's just like the food back at school."

Ashley pushed her plate away and picked up her water bottle. "How about that grocery-store run?" she asked.

"I have a better idea," I said. "Let's hit the beach house, pronto."

Leaving our trays behind, we made a break for it. *Beach house, here we come!* I thought.

"Wow!" I gasped when I saw the beach house that night. Ashley, Chris, Melinda and I climbed out of Chris's Jeep Cherokee and checked out the scene. "This is *not* standard party central."

Fifty or sixty people were milling around a huge bonfire on the beach. A little farther down the beach loomed a hulking, boarded-up house. A band played on a makeshift stage, lit by the headlights of five parked cars. Everybody was dancing.

"What are we waiting for?" Ashley said. "Let's get in there!"

We headed down the beach towards a huge cooler. I reached in and grabbed drinks for everybody. Chris rummaged through one of the brown bags filled with snacks.

"S'mores, anyone?" he offered.

"I'm in!" I answered.

Chris snagged some chocolate, marshmallows and graham crackers. A pile of thin sticks was lying on the ground near the snack bags, obviously meant for toasting marshmallows. We each grabbed a stick and headed for the fire.

"Chris is an expert s'more maker," Melinda explained, handing her stick to her brother.

"I like to think of it as an art form," Chris said with mock seriousness.

"Will you make mine?" Ashley asked. "I don't think I've ever toasted a marshmallow without setting it on fire."

"No problem." Chris speared four marshmallows with our sticks and took them over to the fire. Minutes later he returned and handed us each a stick.

"The key is proper graham cracker placement," Chris explained. He brought a chunk of chocolate and two grahams over to me, sandwiched my marshmallow between them, and pulled the whole thing off the end of the stick. *"Voilà!"*

I took a small but messy bite of the little sandwich. "It's perfect," I declared as the chocolate melted in my mouth.

Chris beamed at the compliment, then made three more for himself, Ashley and Melinda.

"Let's go check out the band!" Melinda said, licking a bit of marshmallow off her lip.

"They're really good. Who are they?" Ashley asked as we approached the stage.

"That's Dan, Justin, Chico and Rick," Chris said, pointing to each of the guys. "They haven't named their band yet."

"You know them?" I asked.

"Sure. They're all working security," Melinda said. "A lot of the people working here this summer are aspiring musicians."

"Yeah, at the end of the summer they have this contest," Chris said, popping his last bit of s'more into his mouth. "There's a huge concert and one of the amateur acts gets a record contract."

"You're kidding," Ashley said, her eyes wide. "So these guys came here to get discovered?"

"And to see all these other acts play," Melinda said. "It's a great place to hear new styles of music and meet all kinds of people—"

"Of course, they do all want to win," Chris interjected.

The band finished their last song and everyone applauded. Then they took their instruments off the stage and came right down into the crowd to watch the next act.

"How cool!" I whispered to Ashley. "Someone here could be a star by the end of the summer!"

"Hey! That's Akiko!" Ashley pointed to the stage.

I turned. Sure enough, the girl who had checked us in that afternoon was walking to the mike with a guitar.

"Go, Akiko!" I shouted, and everyone clapped.

"Thanks... whoever that was," Akiko said, squinting at the crowd.

She started to play and I looked at my friends, impressed. She had a cool, slightly rough-sounding voice. There was obviously going to be some major competition for that record deal. I couldn't wait to find out who would win!

I shivered in the stiff wind blowing off the ocean. Akiko was just finishing her set. I pulled my sweater tighter around my body. How could I be so hot and so cold in one day?

"You guys wanna go for a walk?" I asked Mary-Kate and the others, hoping it would warm us up a little.

"Okay. Let's check out the rest of the beach," Mary-Kate agreed.

The four of us turned away from the stage

and walked along the water's edge together.

A few notes from a guitar floated along on the breeze. I grabbed Mary-Kate's wrist.

"Do you hear that?" I asked her.

"What?" She stopped to listen.

Our ears picked up the guitar again, louder, and accompanied by a voice. A girl's really pretty voice.

"It's coming from that cove," Melinda said.

"Come on," Chris whispered.

He jogged over to the rocks and we followed quietly. We crept around the rocks and peeked into the cove.

Penny and Brian were sitting next to a small campfire. Brian was playing the guitar and Penny was singing.

I watched them, stunned speechless. Penny – the girl who never talked – had the most angelic voice I'd ever heard. And Brian was amazing on his guitar, too.

"Who are they?" Mary-Kate whispered.

"Brian and Penny," I answered her.

"Brian and Penny from the pizza stand? Brian, the guy you thought was cute?" Mary-Kate asked.

"Yeah," I said. I studied the scene – a boy, a girl, a moonlit beach. It was all pretty... romantic.

"Oh, no." I lowered my eyes. Were Penny and Brian boyfriend and girlfriend?

chapter five

"Wow. Brian and Penny are really good together," Melinda whispered.

"They are," I agreed.

Mary-Kate nudged me with her elbow. "You're dying to know – just ask," she said.

I swallowed hard. "Are Brian and Penny... you know... a couple?"

"Penny and Brian? Nah," Melinda said, waving off the suggestion. "They're friends from home, actually. They came down here from Seattle."

"Just friends. That's cool," I said. I let out a sigh. I couldn't believe how relieved I felt!

"Whoa!" Chris shifted his feet and lost his balance. He grabbed at the rocks for support and loosened a bunch of pebbles, causing a mini-avalanche. Brian and Penny stopped playing, startled, and looked up at us.

"Uh, hi!" Melinda said with a little wave.

"Hi," Brian returned. His eyes darted to me and he smiled.

Penny stood up. "How long have you been standing there?" she demanded.

"Not long," I said quickly. "Really. We were just walking on the beach and we—"

"I can't believe you were spying on us!" Penny cried.

"Sorry, Penny." Melinda bit her lip. "But I never knew you were such a great singer!"

"Yeah! You guys should talk to Mary-Kate and Ashley here," Chris added. "Maybe their dad can pull a few strings and get you a record deal!"

"What do you mean?" Brian asked.

"Their dad's a big record exec," Chris explained. "That's how they got their jobs here." He turned to Mary-Kate, all excited over his brainstorm. "You guys should totally call him and—"

"We don't need any help, thanks," Penny snapped. All the colour drained from Chris's face as she brushed right by us and stormed up the beach.

"Penny! Wait!" Brian called. But it was too late. She was already out of earshot.

"Sorry, you guys," Chris said, hanging his head. "I thought I was helping."

"Hey, don't worry about it," Mary-Kate said, touching his arm. "You didn't do anything wrong."

The beach got a little darker. I turned around to find that Brian had kicked sand on the fire, killing the flames.

"Don't mind Penny," he said through the darkness. He walked over to where we stood at the edge of the cove. He looked incredible in an oversized blue sweater and well-worn jeans. He was holding his guitar by the neck. "We usually practice without an audience."

"That's okay," I told him, even though I was still flustered by Penny's reaction. "Brian, this is my sister, Mary-Kate."

"Hi," Brian said. Then he did a little double take.

"Yeah, we're twins," Mary-Kate said. "Don't worry, the moonlight is not playing tricks on you."

"Good to know," Brian said with a smile. "So, your dad works for a record company, huh? That's cool."

"Yeah," Mary-Kate replied. "But it's not like we'd ever know it. These jobs are the closest we've ever come to 'the biz'. To be honest, I don't even think we could help you guys *buy* a record, let alone make one."

"Don't worry. I wouldn't ask you to," Brian said as we followed Penny's footprints in the sand. Chris and Melinda marched along ahead of us. "We're planning to enter the contest, so who knows? Maybe that record deal will work out anyway."

"You guys are really amazing," I said, tucking my hands inside the sleeves of my sweater. "Do you have any favourite guitarists... you know... influences?"

"Sure," Brian said. "I learned a whole lot from listening to some older stuff – you know, from the seventies. But lately I've been really into Glowstick. Gavin Michaels is one of the best guitarists out there."

Mary-Kate and I exchanged a look.

"We love Glowstick," I told Brian. "You definitely have good taste."

"Hey, thanks," Brian laughed.

The noise began to pick up as we walked closer to the party. Penny was standing at the top of the beach near the cars, kicking at the sand. She looked so dejected, I decided to try to apologise again.

"Hey... Penny," I called when I was a few yards away. She looked up and her face paled a little. "I'm really sorry for sneaking up on you guys like that, but I have to tell you, you really have the most unbelievable voice. I—"

"Brian," Penny interrupted, staring past me.

I stopped, confused. I looked over my shoulder to find Brian and Mary-Kate coming up behind me.

"Yeah, Penny?" Brian said.

"I'm kind of tired. Could you take me back to

the dorms?" she asked. She was already clutching the door handle of a nearby VW Bug.

"Sure." Brian shot me an apologetic glance.

Penny climbed into the car and slammed the door. I felt a little surge of anger. What was Penny's problem? How many times was I going to have to try with her?

Brian walked around to the trunk of his car and put his guitar inside.

"What is with her?" I whispered to Mary-Kate, turning my back to the car.

"I'll give you a four letter clue: s-n-o-b," Mary-Kate whispered back.

I sighed and shook my head. I wanted to give Penny the benefit of the doubt, but at this point it seemed like Mary-Kate was right.

"Listen," Brian said as he came back around the car. "Don't mind Penny. She just has a lot of *stuff* going on."

"It's okay," I said uncertainly. But my mind started racing. What did Brian mean by "stuff"?

"Well, I'll see you later, Ashley," he said. "It was nice meeting you, Mary-Kate."

"You, too!" Mary-Kate called as Brian climbed into his car. In a moment he pulled out of the space and was gone.

Chris, Melinda, Mary-Kate and I headed down the beach. I wanted to get back into party mode, but it bothered me when I thought people didn't like me. Especially when they had no reason to feel that way.

"What do you think Brian meant when he said she had a lot of stuff going on?" I asked Mary-Kate. The wind whipped my hair around my face.

"Who knows?" Mary-Kate said. She paused. "But I bet you're not going to feel better until you get her to talk to you."

"Am I that obvious?" I asked.

"Yeah. But don't worry – it's not a bad thing. You just want everyone around you to be happy," she said. "Come on. Let's go and dance."

"Sounds like a plan," I said.

We ran down the beach towards the stage area. Even though I wanted to let the Penny thing go, Mary-Kate was right. I couldn't stop thinking about her. Exactly what kind of "stuff" could she be dealing with? What would make her act so mean?

chapter six

The next morning I woke up early and couldn't get back to sleep. Mary-Kate, of course, was snoring away, and wouldn't wake up until she hit the snooze button exactly three times. When I finally couldn't stand staring at the ceiling any more, I got up, grabbed my bathroom supplies and headed for the communal bathroom down the hall.

The hall was empty, but I heard someone talking in the lounge. A girl's voice. Whoever she was, she sounded upset. Curious, I passed the bathroom and kept walking towards the lounge. I turned the corner and peeked around the door. I froze.

It was Penny. She was talking to someone on the pay phone.

"Yeah, I know. I miss you, too," she said.

I ducked back around the corner. Hmmm... I wondered. Does Penny have a boyfriend back home?

I crept closer to the door. I felt a little guilty about listening in on her conversation, but I couldn't pull myself away. Maybe I could find out more about the mysterious "stuff" she had going on.

"Don't worry about it, Mom," Penny said. She gripped the phone and looked down at her feet. "We'll figure it out. It'll be okay."

So it wasn't a boyfriend. But what were she and her mom talking about? Maybe her parents were having trouble. That could definitely put a person in a bad mood.

Penny started to turn in my direction. I quickly ducked back into the hallway. I knocked my basket of bathroom stuff against the wall and it crashed to the floor.

"Mom, I've got to go," Penny said in a tense voice.

I crouched down to pick up my things as quickly as I could. But I knew it was too late.

"Spying again?" Penny snapped as she hovered over me. "Don't you have anything better to do?"

"I... I'm sorry," I stammered out. I slowly rose to my feet. "I didn't mean to—"

"Forget it," Penny said. Her face was almost purple with anger. She stalked off down the hall. I leaned back against the wall and closed my eyes, wishing I had never peeked into the lounge.

I wasn't any closer to understanding Penny and her problems than before. And now she had even more reason not to like me.

At the pizza stand that afternoon, Dennis taught me how to use the cash register. "How do you like the job so far, Ashley?" he asked.

"It's fun," I replied. "Much better now that I know how to dress for it!"

Dennis laughed. I was wearing a tiny tank top and short shorts and had my hair up in a loose bun. It made the conditions behind the pizza counter much more bearable. Luckily, Penny and I weren't scheduled to work together that day, which totally helped. I couldn't handle seeing her after the argument we'd had that morning. My stomach churned every time I even thought about it.

"Well, I think you have the hang of everything," Dennis said. "I have to go if I'm going to make it to my other job. Tammy will be along in a little while to help you."

"You have another job?" I asked. "I'd think running the pizza stand would be enough work for one MusicFest."

"Oh, it's not for MusicFest," Dennis explained, hoisting his backpack to his shoulder. "It's my regular job. I live in town and work at a day-care centre. I hired this guy to perform for the kids today and I have to be there when he shows up."

"Cool! Well, I'll see you tomorrow!" I said.

"Bye!" Dennis replied, turning to go.

When he was gone, I stared down at the register, reviewing everything that Dennis had shown me.

"Working hard?"

I glanced up to find Brian leaning against the counter. He held a large piece of paper rolled up like a poster in one hand.

"Not really," I replied. "It's a slow pizza day. Do you want a slice?"

"No, thanks. I just ate," Brian said. "Actually, I wanted to apologise again for last night. Penny doesn't exactly like to perform in front of people."

My brow furrowed. "I kind of figured that. But why?"

"She has this weird stage fright thing," Brian explained. "She kind of freaks when she knows people are watching."

"Then… how are you going to compete in the contest?" I asked.

"I'm not sure," Brian said with an embarrassed little laugh. "We're working on it. Penny is so talented, and I love playing with her, but she has to get over her fear or… well… we're never going to make it. And all I've ever wanted to be is a professional musician."

46

"Wow," I said. "That must be hard."

Now everything began to make sense. Penny wanted to be a musician – but she was terrified of performing for people. And she was holding Brian back, too. That was pretty scary. It probably explained her attitude. That and whatever was going on at home... I glanced at Brian. Should I ask him about the phone call I'd overheard? No, I decided. I didn't know either him or Penny well enough to pry.

"Anyway, I didn't mean to get all serious." Brian shook his head. "I... uh... I hope you don't think this is weird, but I made something for you."

He cleared his throat as he rolled the paper open on the counter in front of me. I gasped. It was a beautiful charcoal drawing of the beach house.

"You drew this?" I asked.

"Yeah." Brian stuffed his hands in his pockets and shrugged. "It's just something I do when I can't sleep, and I was up last night, so . . ."

I picked up the paper and held it out in front of me. My mind was racing in a million directions. I couldn't believe how talented Brian was. First the guitar and now this!

"This is incredible, Brian," I said. "Thank you."

"You're welcome. Listen, I was wondering if... you might like to go out with me sometime?" he asked.

Wow! For a few seconds I was too stunned to

speak. "I-I would love to," I finally managed to answer.

"That's great!" Brian's face lit up. "How about Wednesday at around five? We can meet in the quad."

"Perfect," I told him.

"Good," Brian said. "I'll see you then."

I swear there was an extra little bounce in his step as he walked off. I laughed and looked down at the drawing again. I knew exactly how Brian felt. I couldn't stop smiling myself!

"Let's just stack all the rigging backstage," Melinda suggested. We stared down at the huge pile of metal rods we had to move. "I don't know what any of it is for, so we might as well just keep it all together."

"Sounds good to me," I said.

We had just bent to pick up one of the larger pieces, when I spotted Chris walking towards us with a bunch of envelopes in his hand.

"Mail came." He handed a couple of things to Melinda. Then he ripped open a big red envelope and pulled out a colourful card. He read it and sighed sadly.

"What's up?" I asked. "Someone send you an 'I don't miss you' card?"

Chris laughed. "No. It's just a birthday card from my parents."

"Aw! Chrissy is all sad and weepy because he won't be with Mommy and Daddy for his birthday!" Melinda sing-songed in a sappy voice.

"Whatever," Chris said, whapping her arm with the envelope. "You'd be upset, too."

"I know." Melinda rolled her eyes. "Our parents really do it up on our birthdays," she explained to me. "Dad makes our favourite meal—"

"And our mother is, like, a cake genius," Chris added.

"It's kind of a big deal," Melinda finished.

"So?" I said. "*We* can do something special. We'll go to lunch, have cake, sing the birthday song. It'll be fun!"

"Hey, thanks, Mary-Kate." Chris brightened a bit. "That would be cool."

"What are friends for?" I asked.

"Here you go, people! Performance schedule for the summer!" Theo shouted, coming up behind us. He thrust one sheet of pink paper in each of our faces, then moved on.

I grabbed the page and quickly scanned the list of bands and acts. Some of my favourite bands were going to be there! Rave was scheduled to play in a couple of weeks, and Melissa Ryan was coming as well. But what really knocked the wind out of me was one word, right at the top of the page: *Glowstick!*

I looked at Melinda and we both screamed at the exact same time. We ran up to Theo, who was talking to some other supervisors. We each grabbed one of his arms.

"When is Glowstick getting here?" Melinda asked.

"They should be arriving tomorrow," Theo said in his usual laid-back way. "I take it you're fans."

"I can't believe it!" I shrieked. "Gavin Michaels is going to be here tomorrow! We may actually get to meet him!"

"You probably will," Theo said. "Gavin's cool."

"You *know* him?" I gasped.

Theo nodded. "I went to high school with Dave, Glowstick's drummer."

We both let out a squeal and ran back to Chris. I felt like an idiot, but I didn't care. It was too exciting!

"Oh my *GOD*! Oh my *GOD*!" Chris shouted, jumping up and down like an insane person. "Gavin Michaels is *so* hot! I'm just going to *faint* if I get to meet him!"

I looked at Melinda and she nodded. Before Chris could defend himself, we both picked up our water bottles and squirted him.

The attack didn't stop him. He darted away, shouting, "Gavin! I *love* you, Gavin!"

Melinda and I chased after him, laughing the whole way.

chapter seven

When I walked into our room that afternoon, Mary-Kate was on the phone. I waved at her frantically until I got her attention, pointed at my poster, and whispered: *"I have to talk to you!"*

"One sec," Mary-Kate whispered back. "Don't worry! I will not fall in love with Gavin Michaels!" she said into the phone.

My jaw dropped open. Gavin Michaels? Was he coming to the festival? Had she *met* him? Now I *really* wanted her to get off the phone.

"Okay, Jake," she finished. "I'll talk to you soon. Bye!"

"Gavin Michaels?" I blurted out the second she hung up.

"Yeah, he's coming here... tomorrow!" she exclaimed, tapping her feet on the floor.

"I can't believe it!" I cried. "Glowstick is

playing the festival?"

"And not just them," Mary-Kate said. She handed me a list of all the performers for the summer.

I scanned the list. "Melissa Ryan, Rave, DJ Diamond... this summer is going to be even cooler than we thought!" I said.

Then I put the list down and waved the rolled-up paper in my hand. "Speaking of which," I added, "check out what Brian made for me."

I unrolled the paper and held it up so that Mary-Kate could see it. She jumped to her feet and took the drawing from my hands. Her eyes were practically popping out of her head.

"Ashley, this is so sweet!" she said.

"I know!" I grabbed a roll of tape off my desk and hung the picture up next to my bed. I stood back to admire it. "And that's not even the best part." I flopped down on my bed. "He asked me out on a date!"

"Excellent!" Mary-Kate said. She lay down on her bed and rolled on to her side. "When are you guys going out?"

"Wednesday," I answered. "I can't wait."

"Whatever happened with Penny?" Mary-Kate asked. "Did you work with her today?"

"No. But I saw her this morning," I said, my stomach turning. "We got into a fight."

"You're kidding! Why?" Mary-Kate asked.

"I overheard her on the phone in the lounge and she lost it," I explained. "I think there's something going on at home, but I'm not sure what. Whatever it is, she didn't want me to hear about it."

"Wow. This is not good," Mary-Kate said.

"I know," I agreed. "And there's something else. Brian told me she has major stage fright. He's not even sure she'll be able to perform at the concert."

"Wow." Mary-Kate frowned. "I guess that explains why she got so upset when she saw us watching her at the beach."

"Yeah. It's so awful," I said. "This contest could really help Brian get noticed – and Penny, too. But if Penny won't even go onstage, they don't have a chance!"

"Well, we'll just have to help them." Mary-Kate's eyes flashed.

"But how?" I asked. "It's not as if we can help Penny get over her stage fright. She hates me."

Mary-Kate sighed. "Yeah, that could be a problem. But don't worry, Ash. We'll figure something out."

I was glad that she felt so confident, but I couldn't make myself believe it. I just wished there was something I could do to make Penny like me... or at least trust me. Then we might be able to help her and Brian.

But after our fight this morning, I didn't see how that was ever going to happen.

• • •

That evening, Melinda and I were backstage at the Killer Turtles' sound check, trying not to cover our ears. We had to be there to set up some of the equipment, but listening to their screeching music was torture on my eardrums. Still, Chris was out front with a bunch of the staff, banging his head and moshing. To each his own, I guess.

"Mary-Kate!" Melinda suddenly grabbed my shoulder. "Look!" She pointed out the backstage door.

I felt as if someone had yanked the floor out from under me. A bus was pulling up in the parking lot with the word "Glowstick" painted on the side in huge gold letters.

"Come on," I said.

Melinda and I sneaked away from the stage. We walked over to the break table, where Theo and some of the other workers were munching on cookies. Excellent! Now we had a much better view of the bus.

"I think I'm going to throw up," Melinda whispered. She picked up a plastic cup and tried to look busy. People started to file out of the bus. I recognized the drummer, Dave Aikens, and the bassist, Mark Passaro.

And then Gavin Michaels stepped down from the bus. He stretched out his arms and yawned. His T-shirt rose to expose a tiny little strip of his flat stomach. I couldn't take my eyes off him.

Melinda and I tried not to stare as Gavin chatted with some of the other guys. Theo wandered over to them and gripped Dave's hand. Gavin said something and Theo pointed over to the snack table – and *us*. Gavin nodded and headed in our direction.

"He's coming over here!" I whispered, grabbing Melinda's wrist. "Gavin Michaels is coming over here!"

Melinda turned white as a sheet. I was afraid she really was going to throw up. Before I knew it, Gavin was standing right next to us! I could barely breathe.

"Hey there," Gavin said to me.

"Hi!" I answered. My knees felt as if they had turned into marshmallows.

"I'm Gavin Michaels." He held out his hand.

I smiled. As if we didn't know!

I shook his hand. I couldn't believe it! I was touching Gavin Michaels! His tousled brown hair fell in a messy-stylish way over his forehead, and his eyes seemed even bluer than they were in the posters I had back home.

"I'm Mary-Kate," I said. "And this is Melinda."

"Hi," Gavin said.

Melinda just nodded. She looked petrified.

"So, what do you guys do around here?" Gavin asked, grabbing a couple of crackers. "Do you mind? I'm starving."

"Please, go ahead," I told him. I was surprised he would ask. I thought rock stars pretty much took whatever they wanted. "We're stagehands," I said.

"Oh, that's cool," Gavin said. "I bet you get to see all the bands."

"Yeah," I answered. "But, I mean, you're probably *friends* with everyone in the bands."

"Nah," Gavin said. "Sometimes I come to these things and I feel like I don't know anyone. It's like being the high school geek all over again."

Melinda laughed. "*You* were a geek in high school?"

I smiled at her, happy that she had finally found her voice.

"No. I was *the* geek in high school," Gavin said. "I was the music nerd who talked to no one."

"That's hard to believe," I said.

"But true!" Gavin returned with a grin, popping a cracker into his mouth.

"Hey, Gavin! Let's go! They're going to show us around!" one of the guys by the bus shouted.

"I have to go," Gavin said. "But it was nice meeting you."

"You, too!" Melinda and I said in unison.

"Hey, do you want to hang out again sometime soon – when you're not working?" Gavin asked me.

Was he kidding?

"Uh... sure," I stammered. "That would be cool."

"Great," Gavin said, backing away. "I'll see you around, Mary-Kate."

As soon as Gavin was far enough away, Melinda let out a squeal. "Did Gavin Michaels just ask you out on a date?" she gushed.

I couldn't even answer her. I was too busy gripping the edge of the table, trying to process what had just happened. I couldn't believe it. Gavin Michaels, my favourite rock star, had just picked me out of a crowd! And he wanted *me* to hang out with him! This was quickly becoming the greatest summer in all of history!

chapter eight

"So? How do I look?" I asked Mary-Kate. I turned away from my reflection in the mirror so she could see me.

She smiled. "When Brian sees you, he is going to go nonverbal."

"You think?" I asked.

I studied my light blue linen sundress and matching sandals, wondering for the millionth time if I should have worn my black minidress instead. But it was still light out and I didn't want to go overboard.

"You look amazing. Trust me," Mary-Kate insisted. She picked up my bag and handed it to me.

"Thanks." I took a deep breath and let it out slowly. I *had* to calm down. I'd been nervous and jittery since I'd woken up that morning. It had got worse all day long. It was kind of silly, but I really liked Brian. And I wanted our first date to be perfect.

"Now go." Mary-Kate grabbed my shoulders and turned me towards the door. "He's probably out there waiting for you already."

"Okay," I said as I left the room. "Wish me luck!"

"Good luck!" Mary-Kate called out. "Not that you'll need it!"

I saw Brian in the distance and hurried across the quad towards him. As I got closer, I went from nervous to mortified. Brian was wearing cargo shorts, hiking boots and a well-worn T-shirt. And he was holding a backpack. He definitely did go nonverbal when he got a look at me. His whole face fell, in fact.

"Uh... I guess I should have dressed down, huh?" I felt like a complete moron in my heeled sandals and glossy lip balm.

"I'm sorry," Brian said, scratching at the back of his neck. "I was planning on taking you on this hiking trail so . . ."

I wanted to disappear. But I lifted my chin, smiled, and said, "Don't worry about it. Just give me two seconds."

Then I turned and ran back to my room as fast as my little heels could carry me.

"I'm glad I changed my clothes," I said to Brian. "It was worth it!"

We'd been hiking for about an hour. The shady woods felt great on a hot evening, and the scenery was gorgeous.

"This is nothing," Brian told me. "Wait till you see what's coming up over this hill..."

We hiked to the top of the hill and stepped into a beautiful clearing. It was bordered by a stream and an amazing shimmering waterfall.

"This is unreal!" I gasped. "How did you find this place?"

"I came up here for a hike the day after I checked in," Brian explained. "I kind of stumbled across this spot." He pulled a blanket out of his backpack and laid it out on the ground near the stream. "I guess I was hoping to meet someone who would want to come back up here with me," he added with a shy smile.

"Thanks for bringing me," I said.

"Here. Sit down." Brian kneeled on the blanket. He produced a slim box of crackers, a little round of cheese and a thermos of iced tea out of his bag, along with a few napkins.

"This is great." I sat and tucked my legs under me. "It's like a date in a bag."

Brian laughed. "Yeah. Maybe I should sell them down at the vendors' market."

"Definitely the next big trend." I poured iced tea into two plastic cups. "So... you're a great musician, how long have you been playing guitar?" I asked.

"Forever," Brian answered. "My dad's a music teacher and he started teaching me as soon as my hands were big enough."

"Have you and Penny always played together?" I asked.

"Only for the last year," Brian replied. "We played a duet for a music class at school and it just clicked, you know? We knew it was right. I hope the contest works out. It would be unreal if we got a record contract."

I shifted my legs uncomfortably. This contest clearly meant a lot to Brian. I hoped Penny would come through for him.

"Is Penny... I mean, is everything okay with her? Besides the stage fright?" I asked tentatively.

Brian looked away.

"I'm sorry," I said. "Did I say something wrong?"

"I know you guys got off on the wrong foot, but Penny really is a cool person," he told me. "She's just... complicated."

"Oh." I wondered what he meant.

Brian's face softened and he smiled at me. "Okay, listen. Let's not talk about Penny. This is *our* date. Let's kick back and have fun. Okay?"

"Okay," I agreed.

"Oh! I forgot something!" he said suddenly.

He got up, walked over to the edge of the

woods and crouched down with his back to me. What is he doing? I wondered. As I gazed at the lush scenery, a warm, fuzzy feeling settled over me. Brian put so much effort into this picnic, I realised. Every detail is just right. I think I've met the perfect guy!

"These are for you." Brian returned to the blanket with a tiny bouquet of wild flowers.

I laughed as I took them from him.

"What?" Brian asked. "Something wrong?"

"No," I answered. "I was just thinking that I've never met anyone like you before."

And it was true. Guys back home were always trying to impress girls with their cool cars or with expensive dinners and gifts. But where was the romance in that?

"Is that a good thing or a bad thing?" Brian asked, sitting across from me.

"Good." I gazed into his warm brown eyes. "Definitely good."

"Good," Brian said with a smile.

Suddenly I knew that he wanted to kiss me. A tingle of anticipation rushed down my spine. At that moment, Brian leaned in ever so slowly. Just as I closed my eyes, our lips met.

It was the perfect kiss in the perfect place with the perfect guy. I knew it was a moment I would remember for the rest of my life.

● ● ●

"T-shirts! Get your Glowstick T-shirts!"

I smiled at the cute guy behind the souvenir counter in the vendors' area, wondering if he had to shout like that all day. It was Thursday afternoon, the day after my perfect date with Brian. I had a little extra time before I had to be at the pizza stand, so I decided to browse on my way there. I stopped at one of the accessory stands. Something immediately caught my eye.

"These are so cool," I said under my breath, pulling a pair of sunglasses from a rack. They had slim, dark blue lenses and almost no frame. Definitely rocker-worthy sunglasses. Maybe I could use a *little* of the money I was making this summer . . .

I checked the price tag and winced. They were seriously expensive. I guess you pay a certain price for the cool factor.

Still, there was no way I could afford them *and* have enough money for my stereo. I put the glasses back on the rack and hurried off to work.

When I got to the pizza stand, Penny was already there. We hadn't spoken since our argument earlier in the week. I took a deep breath and walked behind the counter, wondering if she'd say anything. Then I noticed a single red rose lying on the counter.

"That's for you," Penny said tonelessly.

"Oh," I said. "Thanks, Penny."

"It's not like it's from me," she snapped.

"I know. I meant thanks for telling me," I said.

Penny turned away. I ignored her rudeness and picked up the flower. I brought it to my nose. I imagined Brian leaving it for me.

Penny slammed a cabinet shut, startling me out of my mushy thoughts. I knew I had to talk to her. We were stuck behind a pizza counter together. We had no choice. But we'd never make it through the summer like this.

I set the flower on the counter. "Listen, Penny, I'm sorry about the other day. I didn't mean to eavesdrop."

Penny sighed. "How much did you hear?" she asked, crossing her arms over her chest.

"Nothing, I swear," I said.

"Well, I don't have a *mobile* or anything, so just… try not to walk in on me again, okay?" she asked.

"Okay," I replied. I was about to ask her why she'd said *mobile* like that when Brian came jogging up to the pizza stand.

"Hey, guys," he said, out of breath.

"Hey! Thanks for the rose," I told him. "It's really pretty."

"I'm glad you liked it." His eyes darted to Penny. "Actually, I'm here to see you," he said to her. "I have big news!"

"What's going on?" Penny asked.

"Well, these big record-exec guys stopped me a minute ago to ask me where stage B was, and I walked them there," Brian explained. "And while we were walking I told them about us and they said they would love to hear us play!"

"Brian! That's awesome!" I said.

All the blood rushed out of Penny's face. "Are you kidding?" she asked quietly.

"This could be huge for us!" Brian said. "But you have to come with me now."

"Right now?" Penny asked shakily. "I... I can't. I'm working a double."

"I'll cover for you!" I offered.

"You will?" Penny asked, obviously shocked.

"Yeah. This is your big chance," I said. "I'd be happy to help."

Penny reached out and braced her hand against the counter. She was shaking.

"Come on, Pen," Brian said softly. "It's just a few people. You won't have to perform in front of a big crowd... like you would at the end-of-summer concert."

Penny darted a glance at me.

"He's right," I said. "If you impress the record executives, you might not have to enter the contest."

Penny looked at the ground and took a shaky breath. "Are you sure you can cover?" she asked.

"Absolutely. No problem," I told her.

She lifted her head slowly and glanced at Brian. She was still pale, but she managed a stiff smile. "Okay. Let's do it."

"Yes!" Brian cheered, clenching his fists.

Penny brushed by me and out of the side door to join him.

"Good luck, you guys!" I called.

"Thanks," Brian said. He took my hand and gave it a little squeeze. "Hey... do you want to have dinner tonight after your shift?"

"I'd love to," I replied.

Then the most amazing thing happened – Penny smiled at me for the very first time. "Thanks, Ashley," she said. "You didn't have to offer to do this so... thanks."

"Any time," I told her. "Really."

Penny and Brian hurried away. I crossed my fingers as I watched them go. Excellent! Not only did I finally have a little breakthrough with Penny, but Brian and I had a second date! And any minute now all of Penny and Brian's dreams could be coming true!

"I *really* have to go," I told Jake that night, pulling on a sandal with one hand while clutching the phone with the other. "I'm meeting Melinda for dinner in about two minutes and I haven't even changed yet. We're going to plan a birthday party for her brother Chris."

"Where's Ashley?" Jake asked.

"She had to work a double," I replied, walking over to my closet and pushing a few hangers around. "So I'll call you tomorrow, okay?"

"Okay. Have fun," Jake said. "Bye, Mary-Kate."

"Bye!" I replied.

I clicked off the phone and tossed it on my bed. "Okay, just put something on," I muttered to myself. I yanked my favourite red sweater on over my head, fluffed out my hair and grabbed my bag.

"Perfect," I told my reflection. Then I grabbed my keys and swung open the door. I sucked in a breath. Someone was standing in the doorway!

"You scared me!" Gavin Michaels said with a laugh, bringing a hand to his chest.

"You? I'm the one who's having a heart attack," I told him. My pulse was racing. Not only had Gavin startled me, but he was looking perfect in battered jeans, a grey T-shirt and a worn suede jacket.

There's a rock star standing at my door, a little voice in my head squealed. *A real live rock star!*

"I came by to see if you wanted to go grab some dinner with me." Gavin pushed his hands into the back pockets of his jeans. A little lock of hair fell over his eye, reminding me of the poster I had hanging over my bed back home.

"But... you were on your way out, weren't

you?" he added. "Great timing, Gav," he said under his breath.

"I was," I said, my face falling.

Then it hit me. The perfect solution!

"What if you come out to dinner with me and my friend Melinda?" I suggested. "I'm sure she would love it."

Gavin took a deep breath and shrugged. "That would be cool," he said. "But I was kind of hoping to spend some time alone with you, to... get to know you."

My knees went weak. Me and Gavin Michaels. Alone. Having dinner together. Was I dreaming? This was too amazing to be real! This *definitely* sounded like a date.

But how could I go on a date? I had a boyfriend – a boyfriend I was crazy about. And, anyway, this was *Gavin Michaels*. He dated supermodels and Hollywood actresses. How could he be interested in me?

"Hey, are you okay?" Gavin asked.

"Sorry," I said. "Can you just... wait here for one second? I need to call Melinda."

"Sure," Gavin said.

I rushed back into my room, quickly dialled Melinda, and explained the situation. She laughed so loudly I had to hold the phone away from my ear.

"Are you kidding?" she asked. "Of course you

should go with him!"

"You wouldn't mind my cancelling?" I said, almost hoping she would hold me to our plans and give me an easy out. "What about Chris's birthday?"

"Please," she said. "We can plan that later. What kind of friend would I be if I didn't let you go out with Gavin Michaels?"

"See, there's the thing that's freaking me out," I whispered into the phone. "The words *'go out'*. I can't go out with him. I have a boyfriend!"

"Okay, girl, chill," Melinda said. "Jake is not an issue here. No one has said the word 'date', right? So it's not like you're cheating on him!"

"I guess not," I said, glancing towards the door.

"So go. Have fun. And don't forget to give me all the details," Melinda said.

"Okay." I took a deep breath and sat up straight. "Thanks, Melinda."

We hung up, and before I could think it through for another second, I walked out of the door and locked it behind me. Gavin grinned.

"We're all set," I told him.

"Perfect," Gavin said.

As we set off down the hall I pushed the last little bit of guilt aside and started feeling utterly, completely cool. I was going out to dinner with one of my favourite stars!

chapter nine

"This is definitely the best burger I have ever had," Gavin told the waitress. She kept coming over to our table every two minutes to ask if everything was okay. She was about my age and giggled uncontrollably. I had a feeling she was another Glowstick fan.

"Really?" she said. "Thanks!"

She scurried over to the other waitresses and they all squealed when she told them what Gavin had said.

Gavin dipped a fry into his ketchup and glanced at the monstrous, half-eaten burger on my plate. His face fell.

"What's wrong, Mary-Kate?" he asked. "Don't you like the food here? Do you want to go someplace else?"

"No! I loved it!" I said. "I just couldn't be any more full."

Gavin leaned across the table, his blue eyes glittering. "Want to hear a confession?" he asked.

My heart skipped a beat. A confession of a rock star? Did I ever!

"Sure," I said.

"I'm kind of a burger-obsessive," he told me. "Every place the tour takes us, I try every burger in town until I find the best one. That way, if I ever come back, I'll know exactly where to go."

"Wow!" I raised my eyebrows. "So is this one really the best?"

"Best burger for miles around," he announced. "So far."

I smiled. I was having an amazing time with Gavin. He was so easy to talk to, and he didn't babble on about his fame. He just talked about normal stuff, like... burgers.

Plus I didn't mind the fact that every girl in the restaurant was eyeing me enviously. I had to admit it was kind of fun.

Of course, the moment I had this thought, a prickly feeling of guilt settled in. I was out alone with another guy, having a great time. And after Jake and I had joked about me getting together with Gavin. How would he feel if he knew where I was at that moment?

I thought of Jake being out with another girl, and the feeling intensified. It made me feel awful.

But it's okay, I told myself, twirling my straw

around in my soda. *This isn't a date. You and Gavin are just going to be friends.*

"Are you sure you're full?" Gavin asked. "Because the dessert menu looks killer."

"Killer?" I echoed, laughing.

"Well, one of the cakes *is* called 'Death by Chocolate'," he said, pointing it out to me.

We decided to split one. As Gavin placed the order, the waitress finally got up the nerve to ask him if she could have his autograph. Gavin didn't even flinch. He was totally sweet about it and even wrote her a personal message.

Gavin was a nice, sensitive, funny, cute guy. Scratch that. A nice, sensitive, funny, cute *rock star.*

Suddenly I realised that it was a good thing that this *wasn't* a date. Because I could really end up liking Gavin. A lot.

"One sec!" I called out when Brian knocked on my door that night. I took a last look in the mirror, pressed my lips together and smiled. Second date, here I come!

I opened the door. "Hi, Brian!"

"Hey," he answered. He was wearing a clean, pressed white shirt and a pair of khakis. It was the first time I had ever seen him dressed up. He looked amazing.

Then I noticed the expression on his face.

"What's wrong?" I asked. And before he could answer, I remembered the audition. "Oh, no. What happened?"

"Penny couldn't do it," Brian said flatly as I stepped into the hall. "She froze up, told me she couldn't go on, and then ran."

I felt terrible for them. If Penny couldn't perform in front of a few people, how was she ever going to become a professional singer?

"That's awful," I said. "I'm so sorry."

"It's okay." Brian shrugged. "I just wish I could get her to see that performing for people isn't that bad. I thought a small group would help, but it obviously didn't."

I thought about that for a few minutes. "Maybe you have to find an audience that won't scare her," I suggested. "Maybe, if she could just get through one performance, she'd snap out of her stage fright."

Brian sighed. "Yeah, but where are we going to find a group of people that won't scare her?"

A thought nagged at the back of my mind. Hadn't I just heard someone mention hiring performers. . . ?

"That's it!" I exclaimed. "I think I have an idea."

"Turn left here," I told Mary-Kate as she drove us through town on Monday afternoon. "We're almost there!" I called out to Brian and Penny in the backseat. I glanced at them in the rearview mirror of the convertible. Penny did not look happy.

"Almost where?" she demanded. "Where are you guys taking me?"

"Just trust us," Brian said.

"Trust you? Are you kidding?" Penny asked, turning to Brain. "You tell me we're going out to lunch and then five minutes into the car ride you tell me you're kidnapping me and taking me somewhere to perform? Why should I trust you?"

"Hey! Turn in here!" I told Mary-Kate.

She made a quick right and pulled into the parking lot of the Lollipop Day-Care Centre.

"This is it?" Penny asked.

"This is it!" Mary-Kate and I announced.

"Your manager, Dennis, works here," Brian explained. "It was Ashley's idea."

I winced. I'd just got Penny to *smile* at me two days earlier and now he was telling her I was responsible for setting her up. But it was true, so what could I say?

"We figured you could practise performing for four-year-olds," I explained, unbuckling my seat belt. "It might help you start to get over your stage fright."

"You guys are lucky I know some kiddie songs." Penny shook her head as she climbed out of the car. At least she wasn't demanding that we take her home, so that was a start.

Inside, Dennis introduced us to a roomful of colourfully dressed, bright-eyed kids. "Hello!" the kids shouted at the top of their lungs.

"Okay, kids. Brian is going to play the guitar and Penny is here to sing for you, so you know what to do," Dennis said.

The kids all scurried to find seats on a big ladybird-shaped rug. Brian led Penny to the front of the room. They sat down on two chairs in front of the kids.

"Okay, I'm going to sing a song for you called 'The Green Grass Grows All Around'," Penny said. "Ready?"

"Yeah!" the kids cheered loudly. She couldn't have asked for a more enthusiastic audience.

Penny laughed and nodded at Brian. They launched into the song, which was fun and fast and had the kids clapping to the beat. When they were finished, the kids cheered. One little girl with black pigtails got up and hugged Penny.

Penny looked up at me as she hugged the girl back.

"Thanks," she whispered.

I grinned. Mary-Kate leaned close to me and said, "You're good, Ash – really good."

"Is this, like, a *normal* Wednesday afternoon for you?" I asked Gavin a few days later. We settled into the box seats at Dodger Stadium with our arms full of food. "Somehow I never imagined you were a big baseball fan."

"I love baseball," Gavin said, pulling out his programme. "But I hardly ever have time to go to a game. I haven't been to one since I was a kid."

"But everyone here is acting like they know you!" I said. Ever since we pulled up to the gate – in a stretch limo, of course – the stadium workers had waited on us hand and foot.

"I'm sure they treat all the celebrities like that," Gavin said. "It's kind of weird, actually. Doesn't it make you feel... I don't know... freaky?"

My mouth fell open. Was he kidding? Perfect seats? Free food? Free souvenirs? All I felt was cool!

"I don't know," I said, leaning back. "I could get used to this."

Gavin smiled. "Well, I'm glad you're having fun."

I took a deep breath as I felt the now familiar wave of guilt wash over me.

What's Jake doing right now? a little voice in my head asked. *You know he'd love to be here with you...*

"It's funny." Gavin cut into my thoughts. "I've been all over the world with the band and no one in other countries is as affected by the whole rock star thing as people are in the U.S."

"Really?" I asked, trying to push aside my Jake thoughts.

"Yeah." Gavin frowned. "One time, in Venezuela, we went to this restaurant and my manager, who is totally high on power, tried to get us a better table by telling them who we were. The guy made us wait *longer* for being so egotistical."

"You're kidding!" I exclaimed.

"Nope. But actually, when we were in Germany, things did get a little weird," he went on. "This one girl snuck on to our tour bus and tried to steal hair out of all of our combs."

"Ew!" I exclaimed, dropping a piece of popcorn back into the box. "Why would she want to do that?"

"People are strange." Gavin shook his head slowly as he stared out at the field. "I get sick of talking about myself," he said. "Let's talk about you."

I shifted in my seat uncomfortably. What story could I possibly tell that Gavin Michaels would find interesting? My tales of evil geometry classes weren't quite as interesting as hair-stealing freaks.

"What do you want to know?" I asked, stalling.

"Well, let's see… what was the most fun you ever had?" he asked.

That was easy – but should I tell him about it? It might sound kind of babyish to Gavin. "Well, it was my sweet sixteen party," I finally said. "It was outrageous."

"What was it like?" Gavin asked, sitting up straight.

I blinked, surprised. He couldn't really be interested in hearing about our party. Still, it *was* a subject I loved to talk about.

"It was... *killer*," I joked. We both laughed. "We had it in this amazing house overlooking the ocean. The decorations were unbelievable and we had this awesome DJ. But the best part was when my parents gave us our car... and my dad told us we were going to MusicFest for the summer."

"Sounds very cool," Gavin said. "It's too bad we didn't meet earlier. I would have loved to have come."

I grinned and returned my attention to my popcorn. I couldn't believe this was actually happening. Gavin Michaels and I were getting to know each other. We were actually becoming friends. Friends with a rock star!

"I'm sure you've been to *really* cool parties," I said.

"Yeah. It's part of the job," Gavin said. "Not that I don't enjoy them, of course."

Gavin frowned and suddenly turned silent.

"Hey, what's wrong?" I asked.

"Sorry." Gavin chuckled. "I guess I spaced out there. I'm just a little worried about something."

"What is it?" I asked.

"Well, Glowstick's contract with Coil Records

is up at the end of the summer and there's a good chance we won't be re-signed," Gavin said. "We're having creative differences."

"You're kidding!" I cried.

"Nope. Not kidding," he said. "So we need to find a new label – the right label – fast!"

Dad could help him, I thought suddenly. *Maybe his label would be interested in signing Glowstick.* I glanced at Gavin. Part of me wanted to cheer him up with that little bit of hope, but for once I made myself bite my tongue. I wasn't about to make a promise that wasn't mine to make.

That night, Gavin and I were making our way across campus, loaded down with Dodger souvenirs, most of which I'd picked up for Jake. As soon as we walked into the quad, I saw Chris and Melinda coming out of their building.

"Hey, guys!" I called out, waving with my free hand. I was psyched to tell them about our day.

But when Chris and Melinda reached us, I realised something was wrong. They both stared coldly at me.

"We've been looking all over for you," Melinda said, glancing at Gavin. "We were supposed to have lunch for Chris's birthday today, remember?"

I felt as if someone had dumped a bucket of cold water over my head. How could I have been so forgetful?

"You guys, I am so sorry," I said. "I can't believe I spaced on—"

"Come on," Gavin interrupted. "What's the big deal? It's just a lunch. This Chris kid has to be a serious baby if he's that upset."

I glanced at Chris, speechless. Obviously, Gavin didn't know that Chris was the guy standing right in front of him. Chris's face darkened.

"Excuse me," Chris spat out. "But I think it's time for my *bottle*."

Melinda shot me an offended look as the two of them stalked off. "Chris! Melinda! Wait!" I called after them. They ignored me. When I looked back at Gavin, his hands were covering his face

"That was Chris, wasn't it?" He groaned. "I'm so sorry, Mary-Kate."

"It's okay," I said. "You didn't know."

We started off for my dorm, but all of my psyched, happy feelings were gone. Chris's birthday had meant so much to him, and I'd completely forgotten about it.

How could I possibly make it up to him?

chapter ten

"Wow! This place is packed!" Mary-Kate exclaimed as she, Penny and I walked through the gates at stage A on Friday night.

"I told you we should have come early," I said loudly enough to be heard over the crazy crowd. "This is *Rave* we're talking about!"

All the shows at the Fest were taking place on huge fields. People brought folding chairs and blankets to sit on. We were hoping for a good view, but there were already so many people in front of the stage, we were at least a football field away.

"Oh, well," Mary-Kate said as she spread out our blanket. "I'm sure we'll still be able to see, right, Penny?"

"Yeah," Penny said. She looked at us tentatively as she sat. "Thanks for inviting me, guys."

"No problem," I said. "Thanks for coming with us."

"I wanted to say . . ." Penny began, picking at a blade of grass next to the blanket. "I wanted to say I'm sorry for being so rude the first week you were here. I just... have a lot of stuff going on."

Mary-Kate and I exchanged a glance. There was that *stuff* thing again.

"It's okay," I told Penny. "I just hope we can be friends now."

"Me, too." She smiled at us. "And thanks for taking me to that day-care centre. It was fun."

"Any time," Mary-Kate said.

At that moment, the stage lights lit up and Rave bounded on to the stage. They launched into the intro for their number one song, "Love Thing". The three of us stood up with the rest of the crowd and cheered. I grinned at Mary-Kate, once again unable to believe that we were actually here.

As Penny started dancing and mouthing the words, I couldn't help noticing there was a little something extra in her eyes. Was she daydreaming about being up there herself someday? I looked back at the band. Maybe the day-care experiment had shown Penny that she had nothing to be afraid of.

"Oh, no!" Penny began searching the back pocket of her jeans. Then she crouched on the ground frantically looking for something.

"What's wrong?" I asked. "Did you lose something?"

"My paycheck!" Penny exclaimed, looking up at me desperately. "I just remembered that I left it in my back pocket. Now it's gone! What if I lost it?"

"It's okay," Mary-Kate said, crouching next to her. "They can void it and write you another one. It'll just take a week or two."

"But I need it *now*!" Penny cried, near tears as she looked around. "I have to send it home to my mother."

I felt the colour drain from my face. "I don't understand," I said.

"No. You wouldn't," Penny snapped, standing quickly. "You've probably never had to worry about money with your record-company dad and your car and your mobiles, but my mom lost her second job, and if I don't send my paycheck home, she's not going to be able to pay the bills this week!"

I was stunned. Mary-Kate stood up shakily and reached out her hand to touch Penny's shoulder, but Penny pulled away.

"I have to go," she said, a tear spilling over her cheek. Before either of us could say anything else, she ran off, disappearing into the crowd.

"I don't believe this," I said as people partied all around us. "Poor Penny."

"Now we know what 'stuff' means," Mary-Kate added. "And it's pretty rough."

"I'm not really in the mood for a concert any more," Ashley said a few minutes after Penny had run off. "I'm going to head back to the house."

"I'm with you," I said, gathering up the blanket. My heart was too heavy to enjoy Rave at the moment.

"I can't believe Penny's family has such serious money problems," Ashley said.

"I know," I replied. "But just imagine… if she and Brian win the contest and get a recording contract, all her troubles will be over. Her mother wouldn't have to work two jobs. And neither of them would have to worry about bills being paid."

"True. But what if she can't do it?" Ashley said. "What if the day-care thing wasn't enough?"

I took a deep breath. "Don't worry about it. We'll figure something out."

We wove our way through the crowd. As we passed by the concession stand, I caught a glimpse of familiar curly blonde hair. My stomach lurched. It was Melinda – and Chris was with her. I hadn't seen them all day, and I still needed to apologise for ditching Chris's birthday.

"I'll be right back!" I shouted to Ashley.

"Where are you going?" she called after me.

I didn't have time to answer. I had to run if I was going to catch up with them. Luckily, Chris and Melinda joined the line at the snack bar. I walked up and slid in behind them.

"Hi," I said tentatively. They ignored me.

"You guys, you have to listen to me." I squeezed in front of them so they had to pay attention. "I'm really, *really* sorry for forgetting about our plans," I pleaded. "I don't know what I was thinking. And I'm just... you *have* to forgive me."

Chris and Melinda exchanged a look and then Chris turned away.

"You know this meant a lot to him," Melinda whispered coldly. "You can't just apologise and make everything okay."

"I'm sorry," I said. "What can I do?"

Melinda sighed and looked me up and down as if *she* felt sorry for *me*. "I'm not sure there's anything you *can* do," she said. Then she turned away from me, too.

Stunned, I trudged back to Ashley, feeling even lower than I had before. "We are not having a good night," I told her.

"They're really mad, huh?" she asked.

"Mad is an understatement," I said. "Melinda wouldn't even tell me what I could do to... Wait a minute."

An idea hit me so suddenly, it felt as if one of those cartoon lightbulbs were lighting up over my head.

Ashley raised her eyebrows. "What? What is it?"

"I think I know something we can do to cheer them up," I said.

The next day I was organising some cables backstage, totally exhausted. Ashley and I had been up half the night making plans, and I couldn't stop yawning. I was in the middle of a huge stretch when Gavin came around the corner, practically bursting with excitement.

"Guess what!" He grabbed my hand and pulled me away from my co-workers.

"What's up?" I asked, a bit flustered.

"A bunch of the bands are planning to have an end-of-the-festival party and it's going to be huge," Gavin told me. "People are coming from all over, there's gonna be great food, music, press."

"Sounds amazing," I told him.

"Do you think you and your sister would want to come?" Gavin asked.

"Are you kidding?" I exclaimed. "Do you even have to ask?"

"Great!" Gavin said. "I would love to introduce you to my friends."

"Do you think I could bring a few other people, too?" I asked. I knew Ashley would want to bring Brian and that Melinda, Penny, and Chris would love to come, too – if our plan worked tonight and we all managed to make up.

Gavin's smile faltered a bit. "You mean like

those kids from the quad the other day?" he asked. "I don't know, Mary-Kate. I doubt the guys would want too many... *staff* people there."

I felt like someone had just punched me in the stomach. Did Gavin think my friends were somehow lower than he was?

"But you can invite your father if you want," he added.

A punch *and* a kick.

"My father?" My mind reeled.

"Yeah. Theo mentioned that your dad worked for a record company," Gavin said casually. "I just figured he might know some people there."

"Oh," I said.

"Or, you know, he may want to *meet* some people there," Gavin added, winking as he quickly rubbed his hands together. "Anyway, I hope you'll come. I have to go and tell some other people, so I'll see you later?"

"Sure," I said quietly. But Gavin was already halfway across the parking lot.

I leaned back against one of the amps and tried to grasp what had just happened. *When,* exactly, had Gavin found out that my father was in the music business? And why hadn't he mentioned it until now?

I swallowed hard, an awful feeling seeping through my veins. Was Gavin interested in hanging out with *me,* or did he just want to meet my dad?

chapter eleven

"Surprise!" Mary-Kate and I shouted when Brian opened the door to our room on Saturday night.

Melinda was so startled, she jumped back, but Chris froze on the spot. His mouth fell open as he took in the room. There was a homemade banner strung from the ceiling that read "Happy Belated Birthday!" and colourful streamers crisscrossed the room. Balloons covered almost every surface.

"You tricked me!" Chris said to Brian. "I thought you had to come over to Ashley's room because you left your wallet here."

"What can I say?" Brian shrugged. "I'm sneaky like that."

"This is amazing." Melinda admired the huge chocolate cake we'd baked that afternoon. She smiled at Mary-Kate.

Mary-Kate clasped her hands together. "Chris, do you forgive me?" she asked.

"That depends." Chris's eyes narrowed. "What do you have for music?"

"Heavy metal only," Mary-Kate replied. She showed him a few CDs. "I borrowed them from Theo."

"You're forgiven," Chris said.

He wrapped Mary-Kate in a huge bear hug. Everything was working out as planned – so far. I was eagerly waiting for Penny to arrive.

"Do you think she's going to show?" I asked Brian.

He glanced at the open door. "I invited her, but I don't know . . ." He sighed. "She said she'd think about it."

Chris turned on the CD player, and loud, screeching guitar music filled the room. He jumped up on Mary-Kate's bed and started playing air guitar like a true rock star. Everyone laughed as Melinda rolled her eyes at him.

"Well, if you can't beat 'em . . ." Mary-Kate said. Then she and Melinda started to dance around to the music, shaking their heads and flinging their hair all over the place.

"This is fun, Ashley! You should try it!" Mary-Kate yelled out.

I had just started headbanging when there was a loud rap at the door.

"What do you people think you're doing?"

I turned around to find Mary-Beth standing in the doorway, red-faced.

She stalked into the room and hit the off button on the CD player. "In case you didn't know, you're supposed to register all parties with the floor monitor."

"Really?" Mary-Kate pushed her wild hair out of her face. "Because I read the dorm handbook – and it said that parties of fewer than eight people don't need to be registered."

Mary-Beth blinked, obviously surprised that we'd actually read the rules. "Well, is this everyone?" she asked, looking around the room.

"Yes," I told her. "It's just the five of us."

"Six, actually." Penny stepped into the room. I grinned. She had come!

"All right, then," Mary-Beth said. "Just… keep it down." She stormed out.

Mary-Kate turned the music on, lower this time, and she, Melinda and Chris went back to dancing.

Penny approached Brian and me. "Hi, Penny," I said.

"Hi." She wrapped her arms around herself. "Thanks for inviting me. After the way I blew up last night—"

"Please," I said, waving my hand. "You were upset. I understand."

"Still, that's no excuse. I shouldn't have taken it out on you," Penny said. "I'm sorry."

"It's okay," I told her. "Just forget it ever happened." I smiled at her, and she stared at me for a second as if she didn't trust me. But then her face relaxed and she smiled back.

"Oh, hey! I have news," Chris announced, jumping down from the bed. "There's going to be a big party at the beach house the night before the contest, and we're going to have a practice concert."

"Kind of like a dress rehearsal," Melinda put in, looking at Brian and Penny. "So you'll get to check out the competition."

Penny forced a smile, but I noticed she paled a bit at the mention of the contest. Maybe the performance at the day-care centre really *hadn't* done the trick.

We had to find some other way to help Penny get over her stage-fright. But how?

"Has Penny tried imagining her audience in their underwear?" Jake asked me over the phone. "That always worked for me in creative writing class."

It was the day after the birthday bash and I had just told him about Penny and her stage-fright problem.

"Wait a minute – you were imagining us in our underwear all year?" I asked. "Everybody in the class?"

"No!" Jake protested. "Just Ms. Trauth."

"Um... ew," I said. I didn't want to imagine *any* of our teachers in their underwear. The whole idea was just gross.

"I'm kidding," Jake laughed. "So what are you doing tonight, anyway?"

I felt a little flutter in my stomach and paused. A few nights ago I told Jake that I was hanging out with Gavin Michaels – and he was totally cool about it. But if he knew I had plans with Gavin again tonight, would he be upset?

I thought about it for a second. It might *sound* like I was spending all my free time with Gavin... but that wasn't exactly true. Gavin had rehearsals every night – and I was usually at the beach house.

Besides, Gavin and I were just friends. Jake had nothing to worry about...

"Mary-Kate?"

"Oh! I'm taking Gavin to the beach house," I told Jake. "He hasn't been there yet."

Now it was Jake's turn to be quiet. I could practically feel his tension through the phone line. My pulse began to race.

"You've been spending a lot of time with him, huh?" Jake finally said.

"I guess, but we're just friends," I assured him.

"So, does this *friend* know about me?" Jake asked.

I held my breath. I hadn't told Gavin about Jake. Why, why, *why* hadn't I told Gavin about Jake?

"I don't believe this," Jake said, guessing the answer from my silence.

"Well, what's the big deal?" I asked, feeling defensive. "It just hasn't come up."

Ten points for lameness, I thought as I squeezed my eyes closed.

"Really? Well, if he's such a good friend, why doesn't he know you have a boyfriend?" Jake shot back. "Or maybe I'm just not important enough to tell your friends about."

"No! That's not true!" I insisted. "I told Chris and Melinda about you!"

The second I said it, I realised my mistake.

"So you told everyone *but* the rock star," Jake said. "What am I supposed to think?"

I had no answer. I hadn't told Gavin, and it looked totally suspicious. So I said the first thing that came to mind.

"Well… just think whatever you want!" I shouted. Then I slammed down the phone before he could make me feel any worse.

"So, how do you like it?" I asked Gavin that night. We paused on the outskirts of the crowd around the bonfire. I wanted to show Gavin how cool the *staff* people were and how much fun we had at the beach house, but after my conversation with Jake that afternoon, I wasn't feeling cool or fun myself.

"It's okay." Gavin folded his arms over his suede jacket. "Is your sister here?"

"I don't know," I answered. I hadn't seen Ashley all day, and I so needed to unload on someone about the Jake thing.

"I can't believe I haven't met her yet," Gavin said.

Just don't bring up my father, I thought. *We can talk about Ashley all you want, but don't bring up my father again.*

"So are we done here?" Gavin asked.

My spirits sank. "Are you bored?" I asked.

"This isn't really my scene," Gavin said. "Why don't we go back and hang out with the band?"

I pulled my sweater more tightly around my body as a stiff breeze chilled me. "I don't know. I'm kind of tired," I told him, disappointed. "Maybe I'll just go back to the dorm."

"Okay," Gavin said. "You can drop me off."

As we started back up the beach towards my car, I couldn't help feeling uncomfortable. He hadn't given the beach house a chance. He hadn't even met any of my friends. Did he really want to get to know me? Or was he a phony?

"So are you coming to the party?" Gavin asked.

I took a deep breath. The party. Right. At that moment I wasn't so sure I wanted to go, even with all the celebrities and glamour and excitement. But I wasn't totally ready to give up on Gavin yet.

"Yeah," I agreed. "I'll be there."

"Cool!" Gavin said. "I can't wait for you to meet everyone."

We got into the car and buckled our seat belts. Jake's face suddenly flashed into my mind.

This is so wrong, I thought. *There's only one reason I haven't mentioned Jake to Gavin yet. It's because I like the idea that Gavin could be interested in me as a girlfriend!*

And I had to admit, if I didn't have Jake, I would probably *want* Gavin to be interested.

But I was crazy about Jake – and I knew what I had to do. "Gavin, there's something you should know," I said. "I have a boyfriend."

Gavin stared at me, the light from a streetlamp shining on our faces. What was he thinking? Was he disappointed?

I gulped. Oh, no. What if he was never interested in me to begin with? Was I a complete idiot for imagining that he – a music megastar – would actually want to go out with me?

I waited to hear what he'd say. My face felt hot. There was no way this could be good.

At last Gavin grinned at me. "That's okay, Mary-Kate. I still want you to come to the party... as my friend."

I relaxed and started the car. I wasn't sure if

Gavin was interested in me as a girlfriend or not, but, either way, it didn't matter.

Gavin wanted to be my friend – and that was cool.

Unlike me, I thought. How could I have hung up on Jake like that?

First thing in the morning, I vowed, I'm calling Jake to apologise.

"Where's Mary-Kate?" Melinda asked.

"She's out with Gavin," I answered. "So it's just the five of us."

I settled down on the edge of my bed with Chris and Melinda and passed them a plate of mini-pizzas I made in our microwave. "Okay, Penny, try to do one song."

"I don't know, you guys," Penny said, shifting slightly on Mary-Kate's mattress. Brian was sitting next to her with his guitar ready. He shot me a pleading look.

"I just want to see if you can do it," I said lightly. "We have to find out if the whole day-care experiment worked."

"Okay. I'll try," she said.

Brian strummed a few chords, and Penny started to sing.

"'There was a time... not so long ago . . .'"

I smiled as I munched on my pizza. She was doing it! But then she glanced over at us and her mouth snapped shut. Brian stopped playing.

"I'm sorry!" Penny covered her face with her hands. "It's like my throat just closes up!"

Mary-Kate walked in and threw her car keys on the desk. She took one look at us and frowned. "What's going on?" she asked.

"We're trying to help Penny come up with a way to get over her stage fright," Melinda explained. She held out the plate. "Mini-pizza?"

"Thanks!" Mary-Kate grabbed a pizza and sat down next to Chris. We all scooted over to make room. "Have you tried imagining the audience in their underwear?" Mary-Kate asked.

"Yeah. That doesn't work," Penny said.

"Ooh! Ooh!" Chris exclaimed, sitting up straight. "What if you don't look at us at all? Like, focus on a spot on the wall behind us or something?"

Penny shook her head. "I've tried it, but I can still see the audience," she said. "This is hopeless!"

"Wait a minute!" I exclaimed, standing up and startling everyone in the room.

I ran to my closet and pulled a flowered scarf off one of the hooks inside.

"Um, what are you doing?" Penny asked as I tied the scarf around her eyes.

"Can you see?" I asked, waving my hand in front of her face.

"No," Penny responded. "I can't see anything."

"Okay. So try it now," I said.

I held my breath as Brian started to play. A few chords in, Penny started to sing and her voice was more confident this time. I smiled at my friends. It was working! It was really working!

Penny got through the whole song, and we all erupted with applause. Penny whipped the scarf off her head, grinning like she'd never grinned before.

"You did it!" I cried. "We found the cure!"

I was so psyched, I jumped up and down. Penny beamed at me, and for the first time I felt like we were actually starting to become friends.

"I can't believe it," Penny said. She gazed at the scarf in her hands as if it were a magic wand. "I knew you were there, but it didn't matter as long as I couldn't see you."

"Not to be the downer here," Melinda said. "But Penny can't exactly perform at the contest blindfolded. The judges will think she's lost it."

"She's right," Penny said, her smile fading.

"Hey, we've come this far," I told her. "We'll find a way."

But inside my mind was scrambling for an answer. There had to be a way to solve Penny's problem. I just couldn't imagine what it was.

chapter twelve

"So… you told him?" Jake asked me on the phone the following morning.

"Yeah," I confessed. "I'm really sorry I didn't tell him before. There was just never a conversation where it naturally came up."

"It's okay," Jake responded. "I overreacted anyway. I just really miss you."

"I miss you, too," I said. "But I'll be home before you know it."

"I can't wait," Jake said. "Well, I have to get ready for work. I'll talk to you later?"

"Definitely," I agreed.

I hung up the phone just as Ashley came back from her shower.

"How did it go with Jake?" she asked.

"Fine." I smiled. "He forgives me."

"Well, that's good news," she said.

"I have more good news," I told her. "Gavin invited us to a huge party at the end of the summer."

"A huge party? You mean a huge rock-star party filled with celebrities?"

"Yep. That's what I mean," I told her.

"You're kidding!" Ashley squealed, her eyes shining. "Why didn't you *tell* me!" She dived into her closet and started shoving hangers around.

"What are you doing?" I asked.

"I don't know if I brought anything I can wear to a rock-star party!" Ashley called from inside the closet.

I laughed, pushed myself off my bed and joined Ashley at her closet. I tried not to show it, but I was just as excited as she was. We were talking about a fabulous, star-studded event here. It was only a moment we'd been waiting for our entire lives.

As Ashley started to lay clothes out on her bed, I thought the whole thing through. It wasn't really that big of a deal that Gavin wasn't interested in my other friends. I hung out with different groups at school. Some of my friends liked one another, and some didn't. So what? And he hadn't mentioned Dad again since that first time... He probably wasn't interested in Dad at all. I'd just overreacted.

"This could work!" Ashley pulled a slim black

dress out of the closet.

"Absolutely!" I told her. "You can never go wrong with basic black."

Ashley held the dress up and stepped in front of the mirror.

"I can't wait to tell Brian!" she breathed. "Gavin Michaels is his idol and now he's going to get to party with him!"

My face fell as I watched Ashley spin in front of the mirror. I didn't have the heart to tell her that Brian might not be welcome at the party. After all, Gavin and the rest of the guys would probably write him off as *just staff*.

"Hey, Gavin!" I called out late that afternoon as I walked on to stage A.

Gavin and the rest of the band were sitting on the edge of the stage, going over their playlist. I walked over to them, determined to convince Gavin to let Ashley bring a date to his party. There was no way I was going to tell Brian that he couldn't come to an event thrown by his idol.

"Mary-Kate!" Gavin exclaimed, tossing his fringe off his forehead. "Hey, guys, this is the girl I was telling you about. Mary-Kate, these are the guys."

"Hi!" I said.

I was flattered that Gavin had told them about me. They all smiled and said hello, and once again I couldn't believe my luck. I was actually chilling out with Glowstick!

Focus, Mary-Kate, a little voice inside my head told me. *You're here for a reason, remember?*

"Gavin? Can I talk to you?" I asked.

"Sure, but let me give you this before I forget." Gavin reached behind him and grabbed a folder. He pulled out a bright blue piece of paper and handed it to me, then jumped down from the stage.

It was an invitation to the party with all the details. I paused when my eyes fell on the date. Why did that day sound so familiar?

"So what did you want to talk to me about?" Gavin asked.

But before I could answer, it hit me. Gavin's party was on the same date as the dress rehearsal party for the contest! Ashley was going to die when she heard about the conflict.

"Um, don't worry about it," I said, taking a few steps back. "I just remembered I have to tell Ashley something."

Then I jogged away, leaving Gavin totally confused.

"So do you know which song you're going to perform at the contest?" I asked Brian as we sat down at a table in the cafeteria. It was fried chicken night – the only night of the week that the food was actually edible.

"We're narrowing it down," Brian answered as he unfolded his napkin. "We wouldn't even be doing that if it weren't for you, Ashley. I think Penny's actually starting to feel like she can do this."

"Well, we're not done yet," I said. "We still have to find a way to blindfold her without actually blindfolding her."

We both laughed, but we *were* running out of time. If we didn't find an answer soon...

"There you are!"

I looked up to find Mary-Kate speed-walking down the centre aisle of the dining hall, her face all flushed.

"What's up?" I asked.

"Big problem," Mary-Kate said, dropping into the seat next to mine. She handed me a piece of blue paper as she struggled to catch her breath.

I put my fork down and read through the invitation, my heart pounding with excitement. I couldn't believe we were actually going to a party thrown by Gavin Michaels.

"Oh." My happiness flitted away the moment I saw the date.

"What's wrong?" Brian asked. He glanced at the piece of paper and his face fell.

"No glamorous party for us," I said brightly. "It's no big deal."

"No, Ashley, you should go to the party,"

Brian insisted. "You want to be there. You were practically drooling when you told me about it," he joked.

"Not gonna happen," I said. "I want to be there for you... and for Penny." I turned to Mary-Kate. "You go without us."

"You're sure?" Mary-Kate asked, looking dejected.

I was disappointed, but my mind was made up. "The stars will just have to wait," I declared.

"Who needs rock stars," I said later that night, "when we've got a whole sky full of *real* stars?"

Brian and I were taking a walk after dinner. Brian had brought along his guitar. We settled under a tall, old sycamore tree in a secluded field on campus. The sky was blazing with stars, and the moon sat low and full on the horizon.

Brian strummed a few chords. "I don't care about rock stars *or* real stars," he said. "I just like hanging out with you, Ashley."

I smiled and leaned back against the tree. The scent of roses floated across the field, carried by a warm breeze. *Brian has to be the sweetest guy I've ever met*, I thought.

"I've been trying to write my own songs," Brian told me. "I wrote this one this morning."

He began to pick out a delicate melody. While he sang, I watched the moon rise in the sky. The air was warm and the field was bathed in moonlight. *This is the most beautiful night in the history of the universe,* I thought.

Then Brian sang the chorus of the song:

"Until I saw your eyes, I never knew
How pretty a pair of blue eyes could be.
Until I saw your face I never knew
That a girl could mean so much to me."

He wrote this just for me! I realised. *It's the most beautiful song I've ever heard, and it's for me.*

"What do you think?" he asked.

"I love it!" I replied. "It's fantastic! You should write more songs. You're really good at it."

"Thanks." He set his guitar on the grass and took my hand. I leaned against him.

Spending the last few weeks with Brian has been amazing, I thought. *I don't think I've ever liked a boy this much before.*

"I can't believe there's only a week left to MusicFest," Brian said.

His words shot through me like a jolt of electricity. He was right – our time together was almost over.

"Brian—" I turned toward him, and he kissed me. For those few seconds, my worries melted away.

I'm so happy, I thought. *I wish this night could go on forever...*

But I knew that it couldn't. Brian would leave for Seattle very soon. I couldn't help but wonder what would happen to us then.

chapter thirteen

"Blindfolds... blindfolds," I muttered to myself. I stalked through the vendors' area on the day of the pre-concert party. We had only a few hours left and we still hadn't found a good way to cover Penny's eyes.

"Why doesn't anyone make stylish blindfolds?" I wondered. Then I caught myself and couldn't help giggling at the silly idea.

Mary-Kate was back at the dorm, trying to decide what to wear to Gavin's mega-party, while I roamed around campus, racking my brain for a solution. Suddenly, something caught my attention and I paused. The sunglasses I had fallen in love with a couple of weeks ago. The cool, fashionable, *rock-star-worthy* sunglasses.

I pulled them off the display and checked the price, then did the maths in my head again. The result was the same. If I bought the glasses, there was no way I would be able to afford my stereo.

"Excuse me," I said to the woman behind the counter. "There isn't an employee discount, is there?"

The woman scoffed at me and rolled her eyes. "Sorry, kid."

I sighed and looked down at the sunglasses. Well, I didn't really *need* the ten-disc changer, right?

Before I could talk myself out of it, I put the sunglasses down next to the register and pulled out my wallet. I could handle having a lesser stereo. This was for a good cause.

The woman eyed the price of the sunglasses. "Are you sure?" she asked.

I slapped the cash down on the counter and grinned. "I'll take 'em."

Gavin ushered me past the tables packed with scrumptious food and champagne glasses. Flashbulbs went off all around us. Everywhere I looked, I saw another famous face. TV stars were chatting with musicians as if they were all regular people. Trina Thurston, the star of my favourite show, *Spencer Academy*, actually asked me to pass her a napkin. I had to bite my lip to keep from screaming.

"So, glad you came?" Gavin asked, handing me a cup full of punch.

"Glad does not cover it," I told him. I did feel a bit guilty about not being at the beach house for Penny, but she had Ashley, Brian, Chris and Melinda. I was sure she was just fine.

"Oh, hey! There's Russell Lawrence, my agent." Gavin waved at an older man with slick, greying hair and glasses. The man made his way through the crowd towards us.

"Gavin! How fabulous to see you!" the man exclaimed.

"Mary-Kate, this is my agent and best friend, Russell." Gavin slung his arm over the man's shoulders. "Russell, Mary-Kate."

"Hey." Russell held up his hand, but he kept his gaze fixed on Gavin. "Well, I'll see you, Gav. Give me a call when you're back in town."

I glanced up at Gavin as his "best friend" disappeared into the throng of people.

Whoa! Talk about rude, I thought. *He could have at least looked at me.* But Gavin didn't seem to notice. He was busy scanning the crowd again.

"Carlos!" he called out suddenly.

Across the room stood Carlos Batista – a huge Latino music star. He saw Gavin and headed towards us. My heart stuck in my throat. Carlos had won about a million sexiest-man-alive awards.

"You have to meet this guy. He's, like, my best friend," Gavin said to me under his breath.

Wait a minute, I thought. *Isn't* Russell *your best friend?*

"Gavin Michaels!" Carlos said, elbowing his way over to us.

"Where ya been, man?" Gavin asked, slapping hands with Carlos.

"Touring," Carlos said. "Europe, Australia, South America . . ."

"I want you to meet my friend Mary-Kate," Gavin said.

I grinned as I looked up at Carlos. "It's a pleasure to meet you," I said. Carlos gave me a mega-watt smile.

"Yeah, well, I'd better go find Melissa Ryan," Carlos said. "My manager tells me I *have* to get her to open for me on the North American dates – so I have to be her new buddy."

Before I knew it, Carlos was gone. I was about to ask Gavin what the deal was with his so-called best friends, but he cut me off.

"I *love* that guy," he said.

What? Hadn't he just heard what Carlos said about Melissa Ryan? He was going to pretend to be her friend – just so he could get her to do something for him!

Gavin pulled some girl over to him and gave her a couple of air kisses. I felt myself growing more and more uncomfortable. What was up with Gavin? Where was the down-to-earth guy I knew?

Had it all been an act? Or was he putting on an act for *these* people?

"We *have* to get together," the girl told Gavin.

"Absolutely," Gavin answered. "I'll have my people call your people."

Okay, that was it. Maybe this snobby, fake Gavin *was* the real Gavin – or maybe he wasn't. But either way I wasn't sure I wanted to be friends with a person who had one real side and one completely different fake side.

Which made me wonder – could Gavin be faking with me? Could he be hanging out with me just because my dad works at Zone Records?

Suddenly, one of the waiters, carrying a tray full of used napkins and cups back to the garbage, tripped and stumbled into Gavin's side. He turned purple when he realised who Gavin was.

"I'm sorry, I—"

"Watch it!" Gavin spat out. "Do I *look* like a trash can?"

A few people turned to stare. I was mortified as the waiter rushed off.

"What is going on with you?" I whispered to Gavin, pulling him towards a semi-quiet corner.

"What are you talking about?" Gavin asked.

"You're acting so different tonight," I told him.

I crossed my arms over the front of the black dress I'd borrowed from Ashley. "Listen, there's something that's been bothering me. Something I have to ask you. Have you been hanging out with me because my father is in the music business?"

"What?" Gavin blurted out, stunned. "Mary-Kate, you have to know me better than that."

I took a deep breath, feeling slightly relieved. Maybe Gavin was just having an off night—

"So, *did* you invite your dad?" he asked, looking over my shoulder.

"Ugh!" I cried out, throwing my hands in the air. "I'm sorry. I have to get out of here."

I turned on my high heels and walked away, paying no attention to the whispers and giggles that followed me. I couldn't believe it! Gavin Michaels was the shallowest and phoniest person I had ever met! And I'd wasted half my summer on him!

It was time for me to get back to what was important. I just hoped Penny and Brian hadn't performed yet.

I clutched the sunglasses as I ran through the crowd at the beach house that night. One of the bands was already playing, and I knew Brian and Penny would be up soon. Thankfully, we had a meeting place, so I didn't have to search for them.

When I came around the back of the darkened beach house, I found Chris, Melinda and Brian standing there, all trying to calm Penny down.

"Ashley! You have to help me!" Penny wailed when she spotted me. "I can't go out there with a scarf around my head! How did I get myself into this? I'm going to look totally stupid."

"No problem!" I cried. I held out the sunglasses to Penny. "I got you these."

Penny took the glasses from me. "How are these going to—"

"Just put them on!" I said.

"Those are totally cool!" Melinda exclaimed when Penny slipped the glasses over her eyes.

In her black tank top and jeans, with those glasses on, Penny looked like a real rock star.

"I can hardly see anything," Penny said.

"That's the idea!" I explained. "The lenses are so dark, no one in the audience will be able to see your eyes, either."

"Hey! You could probably even close your eyes if you wanted to!" Chris suggested.

Penny took the glasses off and grinned. "Thanks, Ashley," she said. "Okay. I'll go on."

Brian let out a whoop of joy and grabbed Penny up in his arms, swinging her around. The rest of us laughed, completely relieved. Penny was finally going to perform!

The band onstage finished up their song to wild cheers from the crowd and then Mary-Beth, who was running the show, stepped up to the microphone.

"Next up are Penny and Brian!" she shouted.

"That's us," Brian said excitedly. He turned to me and gave me a quick kiss. "Thank you," he whispered.

I smiled, chills running all over my body. "Any time," I responded.

Penny and Brian rushed out on to the stage. Chris, Melinda and I hung back. We had a good side view, and I was too nervous to get in the middle of the crowd. Penny and Brian sat down on the two stools in the centre of the stage, and I crossed my fingers.

"It's going to work," Melinda said. "Don't worry."

Chris stood at my other side and I took a deep breath. I felt so much better just having them there with me.

Brian began playing. By now we knew the song by heart. My pulse seemed to quicken with every moment as he got closer and closer to the point where Penny was to start singing.

Come on. Come on, I urged silently.

And then the intro was done. Penny opened her mouth. And nothing came out.

chapter fourteen

A murmur rushed through the crowd as everyone turned to each other, wondering what was up with Penny. Brian stopped and tried starting over, but Penny still didn't make a sound. She was just sitting there, paler than any girl should be in the middle of the summer in California.

And it was all my fault.

"Oh, no," I groaned. "This isn't happening." I reached out and grabbed Melinda's hand. The scene in front of us was horrifying.

"It's gonna be okay," Chris said.

"No, it's not!" I replied as the silent moments crawled by. "I am such an idiot! Did I really think that all of Penny's problems could be solved with a pair of sunglasses?"

As the voices of confusion in the audience grew louder, Brian leaned over and whispered something to Penny. She nodded almost imperceptibly, and Brian, obviously shaken, started to play one more time.

"I can't take it," I said, covering my eyes. "I can't watch this any more!"

But then, when the intro was over, I heard the impossible. I heard Penny start to sing.

"She's doing it," Melinda said, shaking me gleefully. "Look! She's doing it!"

I opened my eyes. Every part of Penny's body aside from her mouth seemed to be frozen. She looked beyond uncomfortable, but at least she was singing. Sort of. Her usually strong voice sounded quiet and strained. I glanced over at the audience and saw that some of them were still squirming.

"Come on, Penny," I urged, trying to send her good vibes. "You can do it."

And gradually it seemed that Penny was realising she could do it, too. The longer she sang, the stronger her voice became. As she and Brian reached the bridge of the song, the audience started paying attention.

I smiled as a few people in the front of the crowd swayed to the music. And I saw Brian smile, too. I allowed myself a little sigh of relief. The ordeal was almost over.

I arrived at the beach house just in time to see Penny singing her heart out on the last few lines of the song. For a moment I couldn't believe it. She wasn't even blindfolded! I jostled my way through the audience until I was as close to the front as I could get. That was when I noticed the sunglasses. They made her look totally glam. She could definitely rub elbows at Gavin's party.

Penny and Brian finished up their song and the crowd went crazy. I couldn't believe I almost missed this just to hang out with Gavin. This was what friendship was really about – supporting one another and being there for the big moments.

And from the grin on Penny's face as she walked offstage, I knew this was one of the biggest moments of her life.

She and Brian headed towards the deserted beach house. I ran after them. Chris, Melinda and Ashley were already there, waiting.

"You were amazing!" I cried as I joined the happy, hugging crowd.

"Mary-Kate! You made it!" Penny exclaimed. She threw her arms around my neck and hugged me so tight, I thought I was going to need an oxygen mask.

"I wouldn't have missed it for all the celebrities in the world," I told her.

"I knew you would come around," Ashley said. "We are *much* more fun than those rich, fabulous, glamorous types."

Everyone laughed. "You have no idea," I

agreed, rolling my eyes. I leaned in towards Ashley's ear and whispered, "I'll tell you all about it later."

"You'd better," she whispered back.

"So they totally loved you!" Ashley exclaimed, clapping her hands together.

"Did they?" Brian asked, scratching at the back of his neck.

"Are you kidding?" Melinda blurted out. She whacked his shoulder to get his attention. "Didn't you hear the adoring applause?"

"I think I'm in a daze," Brian admitted. "A happy daze, of course." He turned his attention to Penny. "You were incredible, Pen. Tomorrow night, we're going to be stars!"

Everyone cheered. But Penny wasn't cheering along with us.

"I don't know, you guys," she said. "Yeah, it worked tonight, but tomorrow we're going to be on that huge stage with all those important people watching. What if I freeze up again?"

"You won't," Ashley said. "Now that you know you can do it, you'll be able to do it again."

Penny nodded, but I could tell that she was scared stiff. I hoped that Ashley was right. I hoped Penny could perform again tomorrow night.

chapter fifteen

"Dad! Over here!" I shouted. I waved at Dad and broke into a grin. I ran over to him and gave him a huge hug.

"It's great to see you, Mary-Kate!" Dad planted a kiss on top of my head. He hugged Ashley, who had run up behind me, and then took a step back to study us. "Is it just me, or do you two look older?"

Ashley and I laughed. We followed the crowd that was streaming towards stage A. One of Dad's co-workers was judging the contest, and Dad had come up to check out the new talent.

"You know, I'm really proud of all the hard work you girls have done this summer," Dad said. "You've really impressed your mother and me."

I glanced at Ashley and we both smiled. "We've kind of impressed ourselves," I said. I thought back to the moment we'd found out what our jobs were going to be – and how I wanted to bail. How stupid I had been! If I hadn't been assigned to that job, I never would have met Chris and Melinda. Or Gavin.

As if my thoughts had conjured him up, Gavin emerged from the crowd and stopped dead in his tracks.

"Hey, Mary-Kate!" he said brightly. I saw his eyes flick to Dad and immediately knew what he was thinking. He wanted me to introduce them.

For a moment, I thought about ignoring him. He was so not worth my time. But then I realised that would be immature. And I wasn't going to sink to his level.

"Hi, Gavin," I said. "This is my sister, Ashley."

"Hello," Ashley said coolly. I was proud of her self-restraint. Even though she was furious when I told her how Gavin had acted at the party, I knew it must be hard for her to be so chill around a superstar.

"And this is my father," I said. "Dad, this is Gavin Michaels. He's the lead singer of Glowstick."

"It's a pleasure to meet you, Gavin." Dad shook hands with him.

"You, too, sir," Gavin gushed.

Somehow Gavin managed to pull Dad aside. I knew he was talking to Dad about the possibility of switching record labels.

"Why did you introduce him to Dad?" Ashley whispered to me. "I thought you were mad at him."

"I am." I shrugged. "But I figure I'll let Dad make up his own mind about Gavin and the band."

"Wow." Ashley arched an eyebrow. "*Did* you get older this summer?"

"Very funny," I laughed.

Dad and Gavin rejoined us. Gavin was grinning broadly. I knew Dad must have set up a meeting with him.

"Do you want to hang out later, Mary-Kate?" Gavin asked, looking pleased with himself.

"Nah. I don't think so," I replied.

His face fell. I turned and walked off with Dad and Ashley. Take that, Mr. Rock Star, I thought.

I sat in the darkened audience next to my dad and Mary-Kate, waiting for Brian and Penny's turn on the stage.

Finally, the MC called their names. The two of them ran out together. Penny was wearing her sunglasses.

Brian and Penny sat down on their stools. I held my breath.

"She looks okay," Mary-Kate said.

I nodded silently. I was too nervous to speak!

Then Brian started to play... and Penny started to sing! She actually looked comfortable. She wasn't stiff or scared or quiet or strained. Finally – she was a performer!

Then, halfway through the first chorus, Penny

took off the sunglasses. The crowd cheered as if she was some huge headliner who got applause every time she moved.

I cheered louder than anyone in the audience. Penny had done it!

The concert was over. We waited anxiously while the judges made their decisions. Mary-Kate, Chris, Melinda and I all managed to sneak backstage so that we could be with Brian and Penny when the announcement was made.

"You guys are definitely going to win," I told them, slipping my hand into Brian's. "I can feel it."

"Yeah? Well, if we do, it's all thanks to you," Brian said. He kissed my forehead and looked into my eyes. I felt a little rush travel from my shoulders all the way down to my toes.

"Okay, enough with the mushy stuff! They're about to announce the winners!" Mary-Kate told us.

All the performers gathered backstage. A hush fell over the crowd. I could feel the excitement and tension in the air as the MC walked to the microphone, an index card in his hand. This was unreal. Someone's life was going to change because of that card!

"The third runner-up is... Akiko Ogiswara!" the MC announced.

Akiko yelped and rushed out onstage to accept her prize. Brian's grip on my hand tightened.

"The second runner-up is... Unnamed!" the MC called out.

The band that had performed on our first night at the beach house cheered and made their way on to the stage.

"I guess when you can't come up with a name, *Unnamed* is an easy choice," Mary-Kate joked.

Everyone laughed, but my heart was pounding harder than it ever had before. This was it. The moment of truth. I looked at Penny and she smiled back at me. She didn't look nervous at all.

"And the winner of the grand prize is... Penny and Brian!"

Suddenly, everyone around me was screaming. Brian hugged me and Penny jumped in, wrapping her arms around both of us. They had done it! They had actually won!

Brian and Penny ran on to the stage. Chris, Melinda, Mary-Kate and I watched them accept their prize.

I felt so happy, I could have burst! Penny's and Brian's faces glowed. They had made their dream come true!

"I'd like to make a toast!" Chris announced at the beach house the following night.

It was our last night at the festival. Mary-Kate, Brian, Penny, Melinda, Chris and I were all sitting a few yards away from the crowd, having a private party. I leaned into Brian's shoulder. We all looked up at Chris.

"To the soon-to-be-biggest music stars in the universe, Penny and Brian!" Chris shouted. He ceremoniously lifted his soda can.

"To Penny and Brian!" we all cheered, clinking our cans together.

"Ashley! Come with me to get some more snacks!" Mary-Kate grabbed my arms and pulled me up off the ground.

"What's up?" I asked.

"Well… Penny told me where she got those sunglasses and I could tell they were not cheap," Mary-Kate said, straightening up. "How did you afford them?"

I flushed a bit and looked down at the sand. "I used some of the money I put aside for the stereo," I said.

"You're kidding me!" Mary-Kate blurted out. "Ashley, you've been salivating over that stereo all summer!"

"So what? Maybe I'll get a part-time job when we get home." I shrugged. "Besides, helping Brian and Penny get that contract was much more important."

"I can't believe you did that," someone behind me said.

I recognised the voice and froze. It was Brian – and he'd overheard everything we said.

"It's no big deal," I insisted.

"Ashley... you're amazing," Brian said, taking my hand in his.

"That's my cue to leave," Mary-Kate joked, jogging away.

"You want to go for a walk?" I asked Brian.

"Yeah," he said.

We strolled down to the water along the surf, leaving the party behind us. For a few minutes, neither of us spoke. I felt happy just being with him.

Finally, Brian stopped. "I don't know what to say... except thank you. I know you really wanted that stereo, and what you did—"

"It's okay," I said. "I wanted to do it."

Brian leaned in and kissed me. It was an amazing kiss, but inside I felt as if my heart were breaking.

Brian was a special guy – the first guy I'd ever really liked. And tomorrow I was going to have to leave him. What if I never saw him again?

"You are such a cool person, Ashley," Brian said. "I've never met anyone like you before." He paused. "I – I like you so much. I don't want to go back home to Seattle." He looked deep into my eyes. "I'm really going to miss you."

"I'm going to miss you, too," I said.

Brian wrapped his arms around me. I felt warm and happy as he hugged me tightly.

"Listen, Seattle isn't that far away," he said. "Maybe I can come and see you. You know – drive down the coast or something? And there's always the phone, and e-mail, and—"

"But it won't be the same," I interrupted. "It won't be the same as having you here with me."

I took a step away from him. "When you're a big rock star, will you send me tickets to all your shows?"

Brian smiled. "Definitely."

We held hands and walked back to our friends. Dad was hanging out nearby with some other record-company people, enjoying the party.

Mary-Kate ran up to me and tapped me on the shoulder. "Dad's leaving right after the fireworks," she told me. "Let's thank him again before he goes."

Mary-Kate and I ran over to Dad. "Hey, girls," he said.

"Dad – we just wanted to thank you again..." I began.

"For setting up the best summer we've ever had!" Mary-Kate finished.

Dad put an arm over each of our shoulders. "My pleasure, girls. I'm glad you had a good time."

"Mark? Is that you?" A tall, grey-haired man about Dad's age approached us. "It's so dark out here, I wasn't sure it was you."

"Don!" Dad reached out and shook the man's hand. "Great to see you! Girls, this is a friend of mine, Don Maneri. We've worked on a lot of music videos together. Don, I'd like you to meet my daughters, Mary-Kate and Ashley."

"Hey, I've heard a lot about you girls," Don said. "Every time I see your dad, he's got new wallet photos of you."

We laughed and shook his hand.

"What brings you here, Don?" Dad asked. "Working with one of the bands?"

"Actually, I've branched out," Don told us. "I'm doing feature-length movies now. I'm casting my next project with unknowns, and I thought MusicFest would be a great place to find new talent." He looked at me and Mary-Kate. Then he blinked and looked harder at us. "How old are you girls?" he asked us.

"Sixteen," I answered.

"I can't believe it. That's perfect!" he cried. "I've got a part for sixteen-year-old sisters. Would you two like to audition?"

Mary-Kate and I exchanged excited glances. "Audition? For a part in a movie?"

"Hold on, girls," Dad said. "I don't know, Don…"

"We start shooting in August," Don said. "Just for a few weeks. It'll be over by the time school starts."

"Please, Dad!" I begged. "It would be so cool!"

"It's a big part, too," Don told us.

"Really?" Mary-Kate cried. "Oh, Dad, this is so exciting! We have to do this!"

"Well, we'll discuss it," Dad said. "But it does sound like a great experience..."

Mary-Kate and I nodded at each other. "Yes!" We knocked our fists together.

"Hold on girls," Dad said. "Don't start celebrating yet. You still have to get through the audition."

"We know," Mary-Kate said. "But we're going to be perfect for those roles. Just wait and see!"

Kaboom! I glanced up. The fireworks were starting.

"See you later, Dad." We kissed him and waved goodbye to Don. Then we hurried across the sand to join our friends for the fireworks.

We all oohed and aahed. I looked at each of our new friends, Chris, Melinda, Penny and Brian, wanting to remember this night forever.

The fireworks ended with the brightest, loudest finale ever. My friends cheered their hearts out.

"I already thought this summer was amazing," I told Mary-Kate. "But it's not over yet."

Mary-Kate nodded. "And it's going to get even better – *if* we can ace those auditions!"

mary-kateandashley

TWO of a kind ™

Coming soon – can you collect them all?

HarperCollins*Entertainment*

mary-kateandashley.com
AOL Keyword: mary-kateandashley

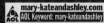

Mary-Kate and Ashley's latest exciting movie adventure

Available to own
on video and DVD VIDEO
29th July 2002

DUALSTAR
VIDEO

mary-kateandashley.com
AOL Keyword: mary-kateandashley

It's
What
YOU
Watch!

Mary-Kate and Ashley Sweet 16

PlayStation 2 — Mary-Kate and Ashley Sweet 16

GAME BOY ADVANCE — Mary-Kate and Ashley Sweet 16

GAMECUBE — Mary-Kate and Ashley Sweet 16

DUALSTAR
INTERACTIVE

Games for Girls

mary-kateandashley.com
AOL Keyword: mary-kateandashley

CLUB Acclaim

Real Books for Real Girls

It's What YOU Read™

b the 1st 2 kno
mary-kateandashley

REGISTER 4 THE HARPERCOLLINS AND MK&ASH TEXT CLUB AND KEEP UP2 D8 WITH THE L8EST MK&ASH BOOK NEWS AND MORE.

SIMPLY TEXT SS, FOLLOWED BY YOUR GENDER (M/F), DATE OF BIRTH (DD/MM/YY) AND POSTCODE TO: 07786277301.

SO, IF YOU ARE A GIRL BORN ON THE 12TH MARCH 1986 AND LIVE IN THE POSTCODE DISTRICT RG19 YOUR MESSAGE WOULD LOOK LIKE THIS: SSF120386RG19.

IF YOU ARE UNDER 14 YEARS WE WILL NEED YOUR PARENTS' OR GUARDIANS' PERMISSION FOR US TO CONTACT YOU. PLEASE ADD THE LETTER 'G' TO THE END OF YOUR MESSAGE TO SHOW YOU HAVE YOUR PARENTS' CONSENT. LIKE THIS: SSF120386RG19G.

HarperCollins*Entertainment*

PARACHUTE PRESS

DUALSTAR PUBLICATIONS

mary-kateandashley.com
AOL Keyword: mary-kateandashley

TM & © 2002 Dualstar Entertainment Group, L.L.C.

Order Form

To order direct from the publishers, just make a list of the titles you want and fill in the form below:

Name   Danielle   Fitzpatrick ....

Address ....

....

....

Send to: Dept 6, HarperCollins Publishers Ltd, Westerhill Road, Bishopbriggs, Glasgow G64 2QT.

Please enclose a cheque or postal order to the value of the cover price, plus:

UK & BFPO: Add £1.00 for the first book, and 25p per copy for each additional book ordered.

Overseas and Eire: Add £2.95 service charge. Books will be sent by surface mail but quotes for airmail despatch will be given on request.

A 24-hour telephone ordering service is available to holders of Visa, MasterCard, Amex or Switch cards on 0141- 772 2281.

Collins

An *Imprint* of HarperCollins*Publishers*

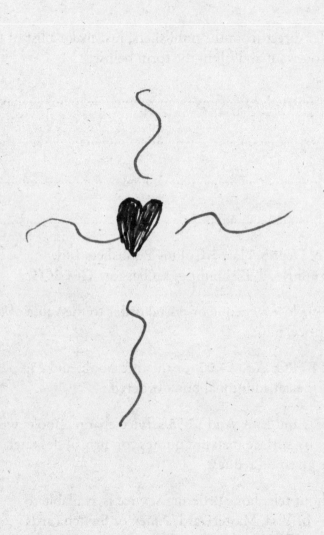